FADE into the
WOODWORK

By
Kristina Circelli

"A heart-pounding, breath-stopping, and powerfully written story, Fade into the Woodwork takes us deep into the belly of fear and then spits us back out again. With stunning imagery, brutally raw emotions, and a gripping plot-line, this story will leave readers peering into the shadows and sleeping with the lights on. Kudos to Kristina Circelli for such an incredibly gripping and hair-raising ride."

-Kristi Strong, Author of the *Land of Kaldalangra* Series

For Rodney
Who Taught Me to Be Independent, Stay Strong, and
always Kick Bad Guy Ass

PROLOGUE

HE SAW HER from afar – an everyday woman in an everyday sundress with an everyday smirk. There was nothing spectacular about her that he could note. Curly black hair that bounced around her shoulders, a small nose that others would probably call cute, golden skin that hinted at a mixed heritage, and a strut that suggested she was as confident as she was cute.

The woman was attractive in her own right, and the rings on her left hand suggested that someone else thought so as well. But he didn't care about beauty. He wasn't looking for attractive or cute or confident. He was looking for convenience, and this everyday woman was about to find herself in a not-so-everyday situation.

He moved quickly, following her discreetly, knowing she would soon be alone. Women like her, with their self-assured walk and bitch-face grimace, usually preferred their own company. He detested them for their confidence and enjoyed watching them fall, even if it wasn't by his own hand.

No, he was just the watcher, the taker. The other, the one who scared the hell out of the man, was the destroyer. And like all the women before this one, she too would suffer his wrath.

Chapter ONE

SHE HATED NIGHTS like these, when she felt completely alone in a seemingly empty world. The sky was black when she left work, the normally bright stars blanketed with the threat of an impending storm. The dim red lights from the botanical shop behind her did little to soothe Valentina Murdoch's nerves as she hurried to her truck, the lone vehicle in the expansive shopping center parking lot.

Such nights, when she rushed to her vehicle while fighting a shiver up her spine, came often, as she worked late in a town that didn't typically stay up past dusk. On this night, the streets were empty, local residents tucked away securely in their homes to wait out the coming rain. The wind was harsh, blowing through the black curls that framed her heart-shaped face, causing her hazel-hued eyes to narrow against the bitter air.

What struck her as worst of all was that the world around her was cloaked in silence. Not even the tiniest of creatures dared to greet her as she crossed the parking lot, as though something else, something bigger and more dangerous, frightened them into wordlessness.

She jumped at nothing, a shadow flickering across the pavement. The feeling of being watched settled over her, sending a shiver up her spine, causing her to look around suspiciously and take in every dark space. Her mind was known to play tricks on her, courtesy of watching too many movies.

He's out there.

There was no one lurking in the night. She tried to convince herself of that fact as she quickened her pace.

Someone might be watching you.

Valentina cursed her inner voice, hating how cowardly she sounded. That voice had taunted her since she was a child, revealing her deepest fears, her biggest regrets, and sometimes, truths she didn't want to face. Even when things were going well, her mind refused to quiet itself against doubt.

Remember the chick in Taken? *She never suspected anything either.*

"Get it together, you loon," she muttered under her breath, taking out her keys. "The Midnight Man isn't out tonight."

Valentina was a small and curvy woman, short in stature and minuscule in muscle, but few would call her weak. Skittish, perhaps, she mused as she quickened her pace, but not weak. She prided herself on her eagerness to try new things, to be the first to leap off the cliffside and into the waiting river below, but it was no secret that she was terrified of the dark.

A sigh of relief escaped when she slid into the driver's seat and closed the door behind her, locking it automatically, as was her habit. The energetic sounds of the Punch Brothers disrupted the night's silence as she started the truck, casting a final look at her shop before pulling out of the parking lot. As she did every evening, Valentina smiled, still amazed after three years that the shop filled with colorful fauna was actually hers.

She often liked to reflect on the days before she officially opened *Planting Roots*. So many told her it was a silly investment while others, including her mother, scoffed at her hopes of securing a business loan considering her pitiful income as a restaurant hostess. Only her husband had believed in her, encouraging her to follow her dreams and pursue the one thing that made her happiest of all – growing gardens.

Their home was testament to that passion, with a backyard filled with rows of vegetables and a budding orchard, a front yard of wildflower beds, and trays of herbs lining the kitchen windows. She took pride in her crop, whether edible or not, and enjoyed learning new tricks to keep plants healthy and bountiful. It had always been her dream to help others do the same, so when the shop space opened up, she jumped at the chance to fulfill that lifelong goal.

She spent weeks perfecting the store, painting the walls a cheery yellow and selecting just the right racks to hold her prized plants. Some came from her own gardens, others from nurseries and distributors she knew only offered premium crop. When it was finally time to open *Planting Roots*, she felt like she was doing just that – carving out her little place in the world.

Valentina's musings were cut short as she reached her destination – a hole-in-the-wall tavern where her friends and husband were waiting. They met there once a month for drinks, catching up on one another's lives before going back to their own day-to-day activities. There was nothing particularly special about the place, except that it served up good food, great drinks, and even better company. Besides, the monthly meet-ups had become tradition.

She made it inside just as the skies opened, sending down sheets of freezing rain. They were accustomed to such weather in their small Oregon town, but Valentina still preferred the summer's heat over rain and cold. Her plants grew best in the spring and summer, but more than that, she thrived on the feel of the sun against her normally golden skin. If she couldn't be outside or surrounded by her plants, then life just felt a little too drab for her.

"My, oh my, is the ever-on-time Valentina Murdoch actually a few minutes late?" a voice to her right called out. "Did The Midnight Man keep you away?"

Valentina turned to the source of the call, a smirk forming across her full, and rarely painted, lips. She never should have told them, any of them, of her childhood name for the boogeyman, considering they mocked her with that knowledge at every chance available.

The Midnight Man was the reason she feared the dark – a cloaked figure that haunted her childhood nightmares, one that lurked in the shadows, a dark and dangerous man waiting for the perfect opportunity to tear her apart. The nightmares began the night of her father's death, a senseless crime at the hands of a faceless, nameless murderer who wanted money and took a life instead.

Over the years, and many therapy sessions later, The Midnight Man finally faded away into the shadows, though even at twenty-five Valentina still slept with a nightlight and searched dark corners for lurking nightmares. Though she'd never admit it to her friends, she couldn't shake the shivers that ran up her spine when she stood in the black of night.

Shaking off that shiver now, she faced her cat-caller with narrowed eyes. "Maybe The Midnight Man has smoother moves than you, Leo Murdoch." Her smirk changed to a grin when her friends burst into laughter and her husband, a tall, lanky man with thick brown hair and warm green eyes, scooped her into a hug. She took a moment to wipe a finger down the lens of his glasses, then lifted a brow when he huffed at the smudge. "That's what you get for teasing me."

"I do it out of love, my darling."

"Oh, barf," a second voice chimed in, thickly accented

with a native New York tongue. The slender nightclub bartender, aptly nicknamed Slim and rarely called by her birthright, Selena, waved at the couple with a bothered hand. "Tina, be a normal wife and tell him he ain't getting laid unless he's nice to you."

"Well, I wouldn't want to punish myself too, now would I?" Valentina grinned at her friend, though Leo became fascinated with the floor in an attempt to hide the blush that was creeping through his cheeks.

"Might as well enjoy it while you can," Slim's husband, Dom, put in. He was a fitting match for his wife – both toned and energetic, both fiercely honest and willing to say what was on their mind. They even looked alike, sharing the same golden hair and dark eyes. "It all comes to a screeching halt once the kids come along."

Valentina accepted the beer that Leo ordered for her, taking a seat at their usual booth. "Good thing we aren't having any then, huh?"

Slim sat back after grabbing another beer from the bar, enjoying her night off from the club and being served for once, instead of serving others. "Still preaching that, huh? Just you wait. Tough-guy Dom over here said the same thing, and now he's a big pushover whenever the kid wants something."

"Am not."

"Are too and don't even deny it, loser."

"Okay, okay," Valentina cut in before they could start arguing. "So, are we still on for this weekend? Movie marathon at the drive-in?"

Slim popped a fry in her mouth. "You bet," she said around the mouthful. "Babysitter is all lined up."

"Two nights in one week you get to play," Leo teased, smirking when Dom gave him the finger. "So are we doing the action or thriller triple play?"

"Action," Slim and Valentina said at the same time.

"That's my girl." Leo slid an arm around Valentina, loving that she wasn't a chick flick kind of girl. In all the time he'd known her, she had always been the type of person who loved being active.

He met his wife fifteen years ago and had been married to her for six of those years. Their family had given them grief for marrying young, not even able to drink at their own wedding, but they saw no reason to wait. They were young, in love, and shared the same viewpoints on what they considered to be the biggest issues – religion, politics, and kids.

Leo loved that Valentina was independent, driven, and a big fan of action movies. Valentina loved that Leo was creative, sweet, and a crafty businessman. They shared a passion for films and the great outdoors, which was what brought them together initially after they met on a hike with their respective families.

Now they continued with their passions, Valentina having opened her shop and Leo flourishing with his novels. At times their friends teased them for seeming to live two very different lives, cooking separate dinners on their own schedules with food purchased whenever they felt like shopping, but neither worried about the other. They were partners in every way, even if their relationship wasn't as traditional as most.

"Hey, earth to space captain."

Leo blinked when fingers snapped in front of his face. "What?" he asked Slim, who had a mischievous look on her face.

"Oh, nothing. I was just telling our girl Val here that Dom and I are taking bets on when you get her knocked up."

He shrugged. "Whose bet was on never?" He saw Valentina roll her eyes at her friends. "We already told you, it isn't happening."

"Aw, come on, man," Dom said with a whine in his voice. "I need another guy in the dad club. It's fun. We hold meetings and everything."

"With beer?"

"Of course. And we watch football games and eat pizza and bitch about how our wives are driving us nuts." He laughed when Slim shoved his shoulder and muttered a few choice words.

Valentina looked over at Leo as their friends launched into their usual bickering banter. "You change your mind on me, you ain't getting laid tonight."

Leo tapped his bottle against hers. "Cheers to that, babe."

THEY DROVE HOME separately, meeting in the driveway seconds apart. Their one-story house was tucked away from the main road, with a long gravel driveway that led through thick woodlands. The property had been in the Murdoch family for several generations, Leo taking it on after his parents moved to Florida, eager to retire in the sunshine on white-sand beaches.

Valentina loved the home, with its high-peaked roof, dome-shaped windows, and double front doors. Last year they'd painted the exterior a mint green with forest-green trim, blending the home with the surrounding flora. She loved the land as well, with sky-reaching trees and plenty of room for their plans of one day raising livestock. Goats, chickens, and cows were top on their list, and part of the barns and coops were already constructed in the back corner of their expansive lot.

Leo had the idea in his head that they would eat what they raised, but Valentina knew she would make pets of her future goats and chickens and cows, complete with first and last names. As a couple, together since they were eighteen, they had made the decision to not have children and so her pets, including their six-month-old long-haired dachshund named MoMo, would be her little ones.

"How were things at the shop?" Leo asked as they readied themselves for bed, jostling one another playfully in the bathroom for sink space. One day they would remodel the tiny room, but for now they managed to fit themselves in with only a little bickering.

"Busy," Valentina said around a mouthful of toothpaste. "Two classes on seasonal crops and a lot of pre-orders for Easter arrangements."

"Business is booming. Never doubted you for a second."

She smiled at him in the mirror, knowing his words to be true. "Thanks. So how was your day? Doing…book stuff…"

"You mean writing and editing and setting up tours? One of these days, you're gonna have to learn what I do." His voice was teasing as he poked her in the side. He'd started his own independent editing company only two years ago, leaving what would have been a secure career in the financial industry to instead focus on his own writing as well as that of others'. His company was still small, but growing steadily. "And it was fine. I signed a new client and she wants to get her new book out by the summer. I've also been talking to a literary agent about my new book and she loved the pitch. We're meeting for brunch tomorrow to hammer out the details. Could lead to absolutely nothing, but then again, it could be the break we've been waiting for."

"Cool. You'll be awesome. I know it."

"I hope so."

Valentina exited the bathroom and approached the entertainment center in their bedroom, scanning the racks of DVDs. As avid movie-watchers, Valentina and Leo both prided themselves on their extensive collection. More than seven hundred DVDs filled the shelves, organized by genre and alphabetized by title. Valentina's favorites were the action movies with fast cars and hot guys. Leo preferred slasher flicks that only attributed to his wife's fear of the dark. But they branched out of their chosen genres when the mood struck, which accounted for their collection of chick flicks, comedies, and classics.

At times, Valentina liked to pretend she was stuck in one of those movies, living an exciting life full of adventure. She liked to think that she learned from each and every film, whether the topic was driving race cars, fending off bad guys, or even cooking a meal worthy of Julia Child. Surely, Valentina figured, she'd picked up *something* after countless hours spent in front of a movie screen.

She selected a dark thriller and popped it in the player, keeping the TV volume low. It was rare that she could fall asleep without the TV on and she typically chose a movie to lull her into slumber.

Valentina crawled into bed, tossing a treat to MoMo when he came trotting into the bedroom. The dog scarfed it down, tail wagging, then looked up hopefully with a puppy-like smile. "No more," she said to him, then flopped back on the bed. "Your furry son is a pig."

"Takes after his momma."

Valentina scoffed and slapped her husband's arm, pretending to be insulted. "Rather be a pig than a naked mole rat."

"That…doesn't even make sense."

"Yes, it does. Not my fault your rat brain doesn't understand it."

Leo glanced at Valentina, brow lifted. "Well, you know what we rats do, don't you?"

"Give people rabies?"

"We make lots of babies."

Valentina groaned. "No thanks, rat-boy. And that was an awful rhyme, by the way."

"I'm a writer. It's what we do." With a wry grin, Leo propped himself up on an elbow and looked down at his wife. "We better start making up for all that sex we aren't gonna have once the kids come."

"Well that's a charming line if I ever heard one." She matched his grin, pulling Leo down to meet her in a kiss.

Chapter TWO

LEO LEFT EARLY the next morning to run errands before his meeting, leaving Valentina to rise alone. She took her time getting ready, making sure she looked her best for her three classes on raising plants that day. Her hair she styled into their usual bouncy curls. Her face held little makeup, save for the mascara that added the perfect accent to her hazel eyes. Her clothes were usual business attire with her own flair – black fitted slacks, lavender flower-printed sheer top with a gray undershirt, strappy purple sandals, and a beaded necklace Slim's sister made for her last birthday.

She loved that necklace, with its flashy amethyst center stone and white bead accents, and saved it for the days she needed that little boost of confidence. Her shop may have been flourishing for three years, but she was still building her confident businesswoman façade.

Satisfied with her appearance, Valentina headed into the kitchen, turning on the living room television as she did so. Her breakfast was quick and simple: a blueberry granola bar, banana, and glass of water. A news story caught her attention as she was feeding MoMo; she listened, absently petting her still-puppy companion.

"Police are still searching for four-year-old Ally Jameson, missing since last Monday. Previous leads have turned up no additional information, though full investigations are still underway." A picture appeared on the screen next to the newscaster showing a cute little girl with golden hair, bright blue eyes, and a charming grin. "Ally joins the growing number of missing children this year alone – the most recent being six-year-old Samuel Beckens, who disappeared from the schoolyard just two weeks ago."

"Shame," Valentina murmured, disturbed by the images of the missing children. She didn't want kids, didn't even like them all that much, but she hated to hear such stories. Her friends often teased her for being a softy, despite the tough-as-nails demeanor she portrayed on the outside, and sometimes she worried they were right.

After her father's murder, Valentina grew up quickly, helping her mother take care of the house and, when she was old enough, the bills. She never complained, never felt sorry for herself or mourned her lost childhood. Instead she faced life one day at a time and took it all in stride, carefully planning for her future and making sure no one ever took advantage of her. If that made her tougher than most, or "bitchy" as had been suggested by others in the past, then she'd take on the title with her head held high. Going soft wasn't an option, not when there was so much more she still wanted for herself, and for Leo.

"No more," she commanded when MoMo went searching for the bag of dog food tucked away on a pantry shelf. The puppy huffed, staring up at her with mournful chocolate eyes that instantly softened her stern voice. "Okay, fine," Valentina relented, hand-feeding him a treat, then washed her hands. "Now you really get no more."

See, you are a softy.

Valentina laughed to herself, knowing it was true. She wasn't much for kids, but she did love MoMo and was content to spoil him rotten.

After cleaning up her breakfast and penning Leo a

quick note to let him know she'd be home after eight, Valentina gathered up her purse and keys. She was already late, and knew she'd be driving into morning rush-hour traffic that would inevitably make her shop open ten minutes behind schedule. It wasn't too much time in the grand scheme of the day, but Valentina hated being late. It was unprofessional and made her look lazy.

She sighed as she stepped onto the front porch, her mind running through the lessons for the day, struggling to push away the tendrils of doubt that still chipped at her confidence. Never one for showmanship, Valentina was still getting used to teaching others and being the center of attention during her classes. She was well versed on the topics and knew what she was talking about, but it still unnerved her to see so many eyes concentrated on her, so many minds eager to learn.

"Shit," she muttered when the keys fell from her hand. Her water jug and book balanced precariously in her other hand as she leaned over, then jostled when a shadow fell over her.

Valentina jerked up, but saw only a flash of black before she was shoved into the door, hitting the wood hard enough to jar the unlocked handle loose. An explosion of stars and pain pounded behind her eyes as she grasped for support, her purse, keys, and cell phone scattering across the pavers. Bracing herself against the door, which had opened a crack, she searched frantically for her attacker.

"What the fuck–"

Her words were cut off in a breathless hitch when the shadow moved again, slamming a hand into her temple. Instinct had her lashing out, connecting fist with face, satisfaction mingling with terror when she heard the shadow – a man – grunt in pain. Her eyes focused long enough to see tidbits of the figure that moved like lightning: a lanky, if not scrawny, frame, poorly cut brown hair, black hoodie sweatshirt, and faded jeans.

A hand fisted in her hair, shoving her head down before a booted foot kicked her in the hip. Valentina landed hard on her back, putting her face to face with the shadow.

"Who... What do you want?" she gasped out, her expression a blend of fear and fury. Valentina kicked backwards, halfway falling through the open doorway, grasping at the frame when the man grabbed at her again. "Get the fuck off me!" she screamed, slamming her foot into the man's shoulder when he leaned over. He merely snarled and kept coming, gripping her ankle and dragging her across the patio, cement scraping at her back as her shirt caught and ripped. Her beloved necklace tore from her throat, beads scattering across the ground.

"Don't take it personally," the figure said calmly, too calmly, as he hoisted her to her feet. "It's just business."

"Fuck you and your business," Valentina snapped, twisting in his hold and doing nothing but entangling herself further. He all but tossed her against a support beam, the side of her head connecting with a solid thud. Valentina slumped to the ground, holding a trembling hand to her temple. Tears burned in her eyes and she tasted blood, a bitter taste that renewed the fight within her.

She clawed, she punched, she tore hair and cloth. Screams erupted in the early morning air, curses sworn at the enemy, blood spilling against white stone as flesh was scratched and pounded. At one point she brought her attacker to his knees, but the fuzziness taking over her mind slowed her down long enough to allow him time to recover. All she managed to think was that, just this once, she hated having neighbors so far away. Surely, in a regular neighborhood, *someone* would have heard her screams and been able to save her from the figure hulking above her.

"You're a feisty bitch, I'll give you that," the deceptively scrawny figure laughed, landing a solid fist into Valentina's gut hard enough to silence her and send her crashing to her knees, cement easily tearing holes in her dress pants. He hovered over her, reveling at the fear in her eyes, the way her breath shuddered. "And you're coming with me."

"No. *No!*" Valentina protested when he lifted her from the ground and began dragging her to his car. Some part of her wondered why she hadn't heard him arrive, how she could have been so distracted and so stupidly careless that she didn't know someone was at her home.

"Get off me, you son-of-a-bitch!" Her body burned with its many hits, but still she fought, shoving her shoulder against his chest and slapping his gaunt face hard enough to make her hand sting. The man only grimaced and flung her short frame over his shoulder. She pounded at his back, fighting against the lines of red and gold that flashed across her vision, struggling to maintain her senses even though her head felt cracked wide open.

Valentina struggled to take a breath, unable to scream or cry for help due to the bony shoulder cutting into her gut. The air spilled from her lungs in a hard gasp when the man shifted and tossed her down, her back striking hard metal. It took her a moment to discover where she was, but when she saw the figure staring down at her with a satisfied grin, realization set in.

The trunk of a car. This was more than an attack.

This was an abduction.

Just before the trunk lid slammed shut, Valentina caught a final glimpse of her home, and had only a moment to worry about the door wide open, and the puppy still inside.

Chapter THREE

A BLACK VOID met her eyes, sending shivers of dread into her chest.

Think, Valentina instructed herself. She managed to rise to her elbows, but her head struck metal, forcing her back down. With her mind racing and eyes watering, she could only lay in place and rack her mental movie catalog for ways to escape.

The fog cleared the moment the car started, kick-starting her mind and body into action. Everything she'd ever read, all the emails her mother forwarded her about personal safety, the many movies she'd watched where this same scenario happened, flooded Valentina's mind. She didn't bother to cry. She didn't take the time to feel sorry for herself. She didn't allow her body to panic.

Punch out the taillights.

It was morning rush hour. She could stick her hand or arm through the hole. Someone would see her and call the police.

Find the escape latch.

Surely she was resourceful enough to find the latch and get herself out. Hell, she'd leap into oncoming traffic at fifty miles per hour if it meant being free.

Crawl through the backseat.

That would put her close enough to attack the attacker

– or have him do even more damage. But it also meant access to the doors.

Kick and scream so someone knows you're in the trunk.

No one knew she was missing, not yet. She couldn't call anyone, couldn't run away. But she sure as hell could scream and let the world know that she was in there.

She had been abducted. Kidnapped. Stolen. Beaten down and taken from her home. That truth slammed into her just as hard as the hooded man's first hit, throbbing in each ache, adding to the bitterness of the blood in her mouth. She had been kidnapped, and she had to fight – starting now.

Taillights.

She could hear rocks crunching beneath the tires, telling her they were still traveling down the long driveway to the main road, giving her little time to complete the first task. Valentina shifted onto her side in the cramped, dark space, feeling for the corner of the trunk. Her fingers touched over fabric, then recoiled when they met cold metal.

Frowning, Valentina reached out again, feeling a hard metal plate where the taillight cover should be. She peered through the dark, seeing nothing, relying on her remaining senses to realize that metal had been screwed over the taillights, preventing her from breaking them. Frantically she reached down and felt for the other light, her fingers again touching metal.

Escape hatch.

Newer cars all had the escape mechanism in the trunk for situations just as these. Was it a newer car? She struggled to remember its make and model as her hands searched the trunk lid, but in her rising panic Valentina couldn't even remember the car's color. Her hopes sunk when she found nothing but smooth surface.

The backseat.

Shifting to her other side, Valentina reached out for the backseat, silently praying for a break. She didn't want to be in the actual cab of the car, within eyesight and reach of her kidnapper, but it was her only shot. The vehicle took a sharp turn – right onto the main road, she told herself – and the jerky movement had her body slamming against the backseat.

Metal. Another metal plate barricaded her in the trunk. Her hands pressed against the barrier, disbelief warring with resignation. This trunk was not meant to be escaped. Whoever put her in here knew what he was doing.

Scream like a fucking banshee.

Valentina had never been a loud person, believing instead to command a kind of quiet respect. But in that moment she let fear and panic fuel her voice, releasing a screaming sound that vibrated throughout her entire body.

The sound echoed all around her, consumed her, terrified her. It was a throaty scream that tore from her lungs, erupting from deep within, her voice breaking at the end. Still she yelled and thrashed about, her knees slamming into the trunk lid, her hands pushing at metal, her back already bruised.

In her mind she imagined her efforts paying off, some unsuspecting driver on his morning commute seeing the car suspiciously jostling about and deciding to call 911 just in case. That image kept her fighting, even when she felt the car speed up and continue driving smoothly, even when no one came to save her.

Valentina didn't know how long she fought within the tiny space, but her fight eventually came to an end. Her body ached and her throat burned, and she knew that hope of a roadway rescue was lost. She had to conserve her strength, prepare herself for what would come next.

And so she lay still with her eyes closed against the creeping dark, calming her breathing, clearing her mind.

She listened to the sound of the car roaring across the road, counted the seconds and minutes until she reached what she guessed were two full hours — all while planning her escape.

VALENTINA OPENED HER eyes when she felt the change beneath her, the car turning off the main road onto what she guessed was a gravel path. Panic threatened to fray her nerves, but she pushed it back, swallowing hard. The trunk was still pitch black, closing in on her as the car slowed. She hated the dark and usually would have had a full-blown panic attack by this point, and supposed it was pure adrenaline that enabled her to stay focused.

Her hands formed fists as the car traveled down the bumpy road, jostling her about. Unable to calm her nerves, Valentina tried to keep her breathing even, counting the seconds and minutes in her head while planning what she would do when the trunk lid opened.

Finally the car came to a stop and she heard the man – her kidnapper – get out, slamming the door shut behind him. His boots crunched over gravel, coming closer, closer, until the key was in the lock and sunlight flooded into the trunk.

Harsh morning rays blinded Valentina as she surged from the trunk, grappling for her assailant. Another scream burst from her, cut off when strong arms wrapped around her gut and ended her flight before she even took off.

"You're right, she is a feisty bitch," a different man laughed, his voice deeper and rougher than the first. His arms were stronger, not allowing her any room to escape. He cursed to himself when Valentina dug her nails into his arm, then flung her to the ground.

The air whooshed out of her lungs as her back

connected with dry earth. Valentina lay stunned, her entire body throbbing. Her newest captor leaned over and grabbed hold of her shirt, tearing it at the collar as he jerked her upwards.

"Get off me, you worthless piece of–"

Valentina was silenced by the knife that pressed against her cheekbone, just below her eye. She could only stare up at the man, her eyes dark, lips slightly parted in surprise. He grinned down at her, a grin filled with malice and a thirst for blood.

"Now you listen here, sweetheart," he warned, his rough voice slicing through her brave façade and bringing fear to the surface. The cold blade pressed into her skin, not hard enough to bite, but enough to make her forget anything she may have wanted to say. "I got orders not to mess up that pretty face of yours, but you fight me again and I'll start slicing everywhere else."

Valentina fought a shiver as he moved the knife down against her breast, the tip of the blade lightly piercing through cloth and into flesh.

"We got ourselves an understanding?" He lifted a brow when Valentina only nodded, her jaw clamped shut as she refused to make a sound. "Good girl. Now," he hoisted her up to a sitting position, her back against the car tire, "what's your name?"

Disbelief filled her and a huff escaped before she could stop it. The man frowned. "I say something funny?" He slapped a hand to the car next to her head and leaned in closer. "Well?"

Valentina met his glare, showing a confidence she wasn't sure she actually felt. "You kidnap me and don't even bother to learn my name first? Why the hell would I tell you now?"

The man grinned again, revealing two rows of yellow teeth. "Don't think of it as a kidnapping, sweets. Think of it as a...relocation, with new friends. And trust me, you want us to be your friends, 'cuz if we're your enemies, then you got yourself a big problem."

He pushed himself off the car and straightened. "You can call me Dane. My partner and bossman over there is Alan. Now, what do we call you?" When she didn't answer, the man named Dane smirked. "Or I can give you a name, but I promise ya it won't be nearly as pretty as your own."

Doubt, courage, and terror waged war within her. She took a moment to observe the two men, casting a quick glance between both.

The one in front of her, Dane, was obviously the muscle. He was tall and well built, forearms and neck inked in colorful tattoos, wide hands dirty and used to hard labor. His hair touched his shoulders in greasy waves, eyes sunk behind a large forehead and surrounded by dark circles. His nose had clearly been broken one too many times, his cracked lips never having seen lip balm. He wore jeans two sizes too big, scarred black boots, and a faded T-shirt with the name of a band she'd never heard of.

By contrast, the man called Alan, with his lanky frame and pasty skin, looked like a certified businessman. His jeans were neat, his shirt clean beneath the black hoodie, his boots nearly brand new. Brown hair was slicked back with gel, face clean of any stubble, eyes a bright brown. But in those eyes she saw the truth – the psychotic gleam of a man who enjoyed kidnapping, killing, hurting.

Both men stood firm in front of her, Alan with his arms crossed and Dane pointing the knife at her face. In the background she saw only woods, great expanses of towering trees blocking any view of the outside world. A small path led through the woodland to her potential freedom – though it could have led to something much worse than what she saw in the other direction: a house.

At another time, in another situation, she may have

been fascinated by that house. The old, weather-worn structure was well placed in the woods, with faded white paint covered by decades-old vines. At least four stories reached up to the sky, a pointed turret on one side and a brick chimney scaling the other. A deck wrapped around the entire home, with wide-set stairs leading up to the front door, which looked much newer than the rest of the house. There were several windows on each floor, all but two on the first floor covered with thick shutters.

At one point the house was probably a warm and loving home to a large family, Valentina supposed. Now, it was meant only for hell and horror.

"Your name," Dane demanded again when she kept observing the structure that was soon to be her cage.

Valentina swallowed hard. "Tina," she answered, glad her voice didn't sound as petrified as she felt. "What do you want with me?"

"Don't you worry about that just yet, sweetheart. How about we get ya settled in?"

Dane yanked her up by her arm, her shoulder throbbing in protest. Alan covered her eyes with a blindfold after pushing her through the door, an action she found ridiculous but didn't protest – not with the knife pressed into her lower back. For a fleeting moment her thoughts strayed to MoMo – where he was, if he got out, if he was safe. Then she forced herself to focus on where they were leading her.

Six steps straight through the door, sharp left. Twenty steps down what she guessed was a narrow hallway based on how many times she bumped into Dane.

A right turn, not as sharp – perhaps a bedroom?

Eight steps across that room, then a door opening to the sound of clanging locks and chains.

Shoved through the door, down a long flight of rickety stairs. Eighteen steps.

Her feet touched hard stone and her nose picked up the stench of mold. Hands gripped her shoulders, directing her to the left.

Another door opened, heavy and thick. The room was cold, and even in her blindness she knew it was small.

The blindfold was removed then and Valentina found herself standing in the center of a square room with nothing but a bed, toilet, and sink for décor. Confusion crossed her features as she looked around.

"Welcome home, Tina," Alan said quietly, then closed the door.

Valentina rushed to the door just as two locks were turned, grabbing for the handle only to discover that it was already locked. Cursing inwardly, she pounded on the solid wood until her palms were raw, alternating between banging with her fists and yanking on the handle.

Eventually exhausting herself with the futile escape attempts, Valentina slumped against the door, closing her eyes to shut out the truth of her new reality: a dimly lit closet of a room that reeked of mildew and chilled her to the bone. There was little space to do much of anything, though she could at least stretch out and stay limber, as she would need to do to remain strong. The walls around her were constructed of a hideous wood paneling, water stained and molded with age.

"Think," she told herself, shoving her head back against the wood as though that would knock some sort of sense or revelation into her.

Two men with weapons, one clearly a psycho and the other the brains. Is he the boss? Just a middleman for...what?

About a two-hour car ride...north? Out in the sticks for sure.

House in the woods, down from the first floor...the basement?

Small room with no windows, one bed, one toilet, some weird mirror thing in the corner, heavy fucking door.

I'm never getting out of here alive.

"Shut up," she demanded, opening her eyes. "You're getting out of here, and you're going to kick those mother fuckers' asses while doing it."

Never one to lie down and accept defeat, Valentina began a sweep of the room, investigating what she hoped would only be a temporary living situation. There wasn't much to see, but she inspected everything carefully anyway, just in case.

Along the far right wall was a bed, if it could be called that. There was no frame, just a tattered and dirty mattress covered with a ratty brown blanket. No pillow or sheets, but she did see a suspicious stain that she worried was blood from another victim – perhaps one who hadn't made it out alive.

Connected to the wall adjacent to the bed was a toilet, and a sink stood a foot away. Both showed signs of age and abuse, with yellow-orange stains coating the base, chipped porcelain, and a slow drip from the sink faucet that would certainly drive her insane if she thought about it too long.

In the corner across from the bed and toilet, placed between the thick wall and crumbling, water-logged ceiling, was a round angled mirror. It reflected the entire room, only a few handspans out of reach for her short frame. Valentina wasn't stupid. She knew that behind that so-called mirror was a camera watching her every move. These people wouldn't leave her to her own devices.

She stared at the mirror camera for a moment, considering whether or not she was being watched at this very moment. Briefly, she wondered if the camera had night vision before letting her eyes continue their exploration. The floor was cold and dirty concrete, the walls an ugly brown paneling, the ceiling discolored. Everything about her surroundings screamed of decay and filth. Only the door seemed updated, clearly reinforced on both sides to prevent escape.

"Okay," she whispered, taking a slow walk around the room. It didn't take long to reach each corner. Goosebumps formed along her arms and she rubbed her hands over them, not sure if the chill was from the room, the reality of what her morning had turned into, or both.

Get a weapon, moron.

With renewed vigor, Valentina rushed to the sink, pulling with all her might. To her surprise, the old fixture didn't budge. She grimaced and dropped to her knees, grabbing hold of the piping and tugging hard. The pipe groaned, encouraging her to continue. She'd just managed to feel a slight wiggle when a voice called out from the other side of the door.

"Don't get any bright ideas, Miss Tina. Be good and step away from the sink. Now," the voice commanded when she didn't move.

Valentina sighed and stood, backing up until she hit the far wall. Her eyes narrowed when the door opened and Alan stepped through. She could see Dane in the shadows, waiting for her to attempt an escape. He nearly blended in with the darkness, but still her glare pierced into him.

"Keep shootin' them daggers, sweetheart. See how far it gets ya."

"I'm not your sweetheart," Valentina shot back, pressing herself against the paneling. In the back of her mind she knew mouthing off would only make things worse, but her temper and fear were taking control of her words. "Where the fuck am I?"

"All in due time, Miss Tina."

"Oh, I see," she said with a smirk to Alan, who stood a few feet in front of her with a bottle of water and what looked like a change of clothing. "You must be the good cop. Sewer rat over there is the bad cop."

Alan's eyes darkened. "Make no mistake, we are not your friends."

"I thought Sling Blade said to play nice, since I didn't want you as enemies."

"Perhaps you should think of us as acquaintances, then," Alan replied, not amused by her sarcasm. "You would do well to remember that we are in charge here, not you."

Valentina scoffed and pointed to her face. "Pretty sure you made that clear when you busted my head against the pole."

"He really shouldn't a done that," Dane put in from the doorway, cleaning out his nails with the tip of the knife. "The boss don't like a busted-up face."

"She fought me!"

"So you hit her in the gut. She ain't big. Bruise up her body, the boss don't care about the body. You better hope that fat lip and black eye heal before he gets here."

Her stomach dropped at the new information. "What boss? Who's coming?"

"The boss is coming," Dane answered casually. "Sometime next week, maybe after. And he don't like a busted face, so you better hope you get pretty again. If you ain't pretty, he won't want you. And if he don't want you, then what's the point of keeping ya around?"

Valentina swallowed hard, but kept her words even. "Yeah? Well if I ain't pretty, I'll be sure to tell him why."

Alan snarled and threw the water bottle at her feet, along with the clothes. "Get comfortable. You aren't going anywhere."

Chapter FOUR

THE RESTAURANT WAS packed with the usual lunch crowd, waitresses hurrying back and forth across the popular sandwich shop to fill orders. Expertly-made wraps and beer cheese soup – the crowd favorite – left the kitchen in a steady rhythm, two of those orders making their way to Leo Murdoch's table.

He sat at the small round table with Angelica Haven, the woman who would decide his fate. His nerves ate at him, but he pushed them back, instead putting on the cool-and-confident mask he'd perfected over the years while speaking at writing workshops. He laughed at the right moments, complimented her on her not-so-flattering yellow dress, and when the time came, gave his pitch his all.

"Think *Pirates of the Caribbean* meets *Snow White* meets *Avatar*. This is a fantasy novel that spans genres, grabbing readers who love history, fairy tales, and other-worldly adventures and throwing them all into one epic series." He couldn't help but grin when he saw the interest in the agent's eyes, and ignored the buzzing cell phone in his pocket as he continued.

"At the heart of that series is a woman, Eva. She's the girl all other women aspire to be. Beautiful, but not obviously so. Smart, with a wicked sense of humor. She's the girl who can hang with the guys but still be sexy. Small, but packs one hell of a right cross. On the outside she looks harmless, but when you piss her off, get the hell out of the way."

His phone buzzed again, and in the back of his mind he hoped it wasn't Valentina calling to remind him of some inane detail or to chat about one of her classes. She knew how important today was. "Clearly, I've modeled Eva after my wife. She's quite flattered, let me tell ya. Anyway," Leo paused to take a sip of water, hoping he wasn't boring Angelica. "Eva is the core of the story, connected to the land she's kidnapped to in a way she will later learn. Upon being abducted from her homeland, she learns the lay of the new world and the people, starts to devise a plan to get back, all while rescuing those who have been held hostage for centuries under a tyrant's rule."

"Why was she kidnapped?"

Leo smiled. "Because she is the rebirth of the one love the tyrant king held dear to his heart, and she is the only one who can free him of his curse."

Angelica sat back, fingers toying with an unopened straw. Her hazel eyes searched his face as she thought about his pitch. She'd already read his other works and knew he was a talented writer, which was the only reason she'd flown all the way out to meet him. What he didn't know was that she had more in mind than just a book, and was interested to see just how creative Leo Murdoch could be with his stories.

After a pause, Angelica straightened. "I'm going to the restroom. We'll talk when I get back."

He waited until she was out of sight to let his smile grow into a ridiculous, child-like grin. For years, Leo had been waiting for a moment like this, that moment when all his hard work, when the novels he'd loved and perfected and published on his own, would take the next step forward, when someone would finally be willing to give him a shot at what he knew he did best – create.

While Angelica was in the restroom, Leo used the time to check his phone. Three missed calls, but not, he noted with a frown, from his wife. Instead, Slim's number stared up at him, along with a text that read, *Call me now.* The lack of an insulting name or teasing emoticon concerned him a bit.

Quickly, he dialed Slim's cell, not sure if he should be amused, worried, or annoyed. Slim picked up at the first ring.

"What the fuck! I called you three times! Leo!"

He heard the panic in her voice. "Slim, chill. What's wrong?"

"It's Valentina!" she cried, and the uncertainty curling in his gut turned to dread. "My sister called this morning because the shop wasn't open, and Val had those classes that she was teaching. She thought maybe Val was sick, so I called but didn't get an answer. I thought I'd drop by before work, and...shit, Leo."

"What? *What?*" he demanded when Slim fell silent. He heard her sniffling on the other end.

"I...I don't know. I got here and the front door was wide open and there is fucking blood on the porch and her necklace is broken to hell all over the place. I called the cops, then you. They just got here and—"

Leo didn't hear the rest of her words. He'd already started a frantic dash to his car.

He barely remembered driving home, but was fully aware of the fact that he broke several laws doing so. The car screeched to a stop at the circular drive, where four squad cars were already parked. Leaping from the car, leaving the door wide open, Leo raced for the house.

Three officers were standing at the edge of the patio. They turned when he approached, taking in the sight of the long, lanky man with obvious panic written across his face.

The tallest of the trio stepped forward.

"Mr. Murdoch?

"I'm Leo. I'm her husband. What the hell happened?" He tried to push past the officers, desperate to see whatever they were all standing around. "Where is she?"

"We don't know," Slim said as she came out of the house with another officer. "We looked everywhere and she's just gone. She's fucking gone, Leo."

The air froze around him as Leo took in the sight. The front door standing open, the wood along the frame splintered, a planter busted into a dozen pieces on the front step. Then he saw the blood. Blood on the wall. Blood on the pavers. Blood from someone who had been dragged away from the house and across the porch.

He struggled to process what he was seeing, what he was being forced to accept. He knew, somehow he *knew*, that blood belonged to his wife. Something terrible had happened this morning, all while he was schmoozing an agent and ignoring her best friend's frantic phone calls.

A bark to his left snapped Leo out of his daze. He dropped to the ground when MoMo emerged from the bushes, dirty and covered in burrs. The frightened pup all but leapt into his arms.

"MoMo," Leo whispered, not noticing when Slim lowered herself next to him and offered a strong hug. "What happened to her?"

HOURS PASSED BEFORE Valentina moved from her spot against the wall. In that time she did what she did best – she listened and learned. She'd already taken stock of her room and everything it had to offer, which wasn't much outside of a rogue roach scurrying through a hole in the paneling. Then she'd listened to the sounds of the house, all its creaks and groans, dull footsteps on the ceiling above her. Sometimes she heard muffled voices, but no actual words.

No one had come back for her, yet. So she sat in silence and solitude, praying to whatever gods were listening that she would find her way out of this alive. So far she had refused the new clothes, preferring to wear her own apparel, even if her shirt was spotted with blood and her pants were torn at the knees. Her shoes she'd kicked off; heels were of no use here. She did accept the bottle of water though, convincing herself that at the very least, she had to stay hydrated. She wasn't interested in being a martyr who refused to eat in protest of being captured. No, Valentina was well aware that she would need her strength to escape, or die trying.

By now, *someone* would know she was missing. Perhaps someone from her class would call Leo, or Slim's sister would call, or any number of people would be concerned that she hadn't opened for the day or informed anyone of a change of plans. Surely at least one person would notice, and be willing to do something about it.

But what could they do? Valentina tried not to imagine what Leo would come home to – the front door open, her blood everywhere, MoMo likely missing. Leo was better than she in emergency situations, more level headed and rational, but this was different. If the tides were turned, Valentina suspected she would have completely lost her shit.

In fact, she was proud of how well she'd handled herself so far. Ultimately she'd still been kidnapped, but she fought like a beast and didn't make it easy, and she'd kept her wits about her. Hours into the ordeal, she'd thought things through carefully. If her directions were accurate, she was in a completely different state, though not far from the border. She was in the middle of the woods, locked in a basement by two men who were waiting for some boss figure to arrive. That meant she had to get out before he walked through the front door. If the movies taught her anything, it was that once a victim was moved to a secondary location, chances of survival dropped almost to zero.

Valentina jumped to her feet when she heard footsteps on the stairs. Instinct had her curling her hands into fists and moving toward the door. When it opened she launched forward, one fist connecting with what she guessed was a shoulder.

Alan was ready for her, expecting her attack, even. He had an arm around her throat before she could react, and she was reminded for at least the fifth time that the wiry man was stronger than he looked.

Her captor snarled as he shoved her back into the room and closed the door behind him, a plastic bag in his hands falling to the floor. "You keep that up, Miss Tina, and you'll regret it." He stepped toward her, pointing with an annoyingly thin finger. "We have to keep that face pretty, but I can still break every bone in both of your feet."

"Your boss will be pissed if you fuck me up more than you already have."

Alan laughed. "Oh, you don't need your feet for what he has planned for you." He reveled in the horror that crossed her face, moving so close that their bodies were nearly pressed against one another.

Valentina swallowed, fighting to keep her gaze even. "You…you fucking touch me and I will cut your dick off. I'll find a way. I guaran-fucking-tee it."

Alan let his gaze filter over her, watery eyes drifting from bottom to top, lingering on her breasts. Bile rose in the back of her throat. If he noticed her discomfort, it only encouraged him. But then, when she thought he actually would touch her, Alan stepped back.

"You don't have to worry about being *touched*," he answered, amusement in his voice. "You aren't for me, or Dane. The boss would be mighty upset if we touched the goods before he did. Although by the end of it, you'll be wishing it was one of us. We're gentler than he is."

Letting that final thought sink in her mind, Alan backed up to the door, never taking his eyes off Valentina. "Now, enough with the escape attempts. You touch that pipe again, and we will break every finger on both hands."

Alan waited until she nodded in understanding, then picked up the bag he'd dropped upon entering the room. Turning the bag over, he dumped out two bottles of water and small box of cereal. "Enjoy your evening, Miss Tina. Come morning, you'll be looking at me in a whole different light."

He shut the door behind him, leaving Valentine alone again. She nearly sighed in relief and was about to let her body relax after the fear of that slimy man laying a hand on her, when the lights went out.

Panic instantly filled her limbs, freezing Valentina in place. Her jaw clenched, teeth grinding together painfully, throat constricting with the effort. She struggled to maintain composure, but her mind raced with memories of the one figure that haunted her.

He's here. The Midnight Man is here.

She knew the thought was ludicrous, but still it persisted, penetrating her mind and turning her blood to ice. Somewhere, lurking in the corners of the tiny room, *he* was waiting for her. Waiting to attack. Waiting to consume.

Waiting to kill.

Valentina slid down the wall, pulling her knees up to her chest. For the first time since she could remember, she was completely blind. Not even the trunk had been so completely, uncontrollably, dark. No light penetrated this kind of darkness, the kind that wrapped around her and smothered her every breath, the kind that was filled with emptiness and yet, pinpricks of icy death.

A whimper escaped despite her determined strength. For a moment, she almost wished Alan would come back, or even Dane. *Some* sort of company would be preferable to the darkness.

Banishing that thought, Valentina reached out and stumbled until she found the mattress. The darkness disoriented her, sending her to her knees as a dizzy spell passed over her. Luckily she landed on the mattress, pulling the tattered blanket from the bed and wrapping it around herself. Knowing it was foolish and that nothing could protect her now, she tightened her hold and curled up in the corner, praying for morning and light.

Chapter FIVE

LEO DROPPED DOWN to the couch, his leg shaking nervously. MoMo rested at his feet, looking up with mournful chocolate eyes, sensing that something was wrong. In front of him paced a stout older woman with jet-black hair that curled around a softly wrinkled face. Valentina's mother looked just like her daughter, beautiful and serene, though at the moment her usual bright eyes were filled with tears of worry.

The day had been rough for them both, as well as for Slim and Dom, who had gone home just an hour ago after the last of the police officers finally left. Leo had never answered so many questions all at once before, let alone the same ones over and over again.

When was the last time you talked to your wife?

Do you have any enemies that may be looking for revenge?

Is there any chance Valentina Murdoch staged this alleged abduction?

Can you confirm your whereabouts for the day?

Though he knew they were necessary, the last two questions burned Leo to the core. No, there was no chance his wife staged a kidnapping just to get away, to escape. The fact that she left MoMo behind was evidence enough of that. Yes, he could confirm his whereabouts and was forced to call the agent he rudely left at the restaurant to prove it. Angelica had been compassionate about the situation, though he doubted he'd ever have the chance to speak with her again. Surprisingly, that didn't bother him. All he cared about right now was getting his wife back unharmed.

He hated being this helpless, unable to do anything but answer the police officers' questions and attempt to calm his mother-in-law. For the past six hours he'd racked his brain trying to think of something, anything, that he could do, but the simple truth was, no one had any idea where Valentina was, who had taken her, or why she had been kidnapped.

Had someone been watching them? All those nights when he teased Valentina about The Midnight Man, did she really see or hear someone lurking in the shadows? He'd failed as a husband to protect her from those things, and vowed that if — when — she came back to him, that he'd never tease her again over such things. He would be doting, compassionate, protective. He would prevent something like this from ever happening again.

"It's not your fault."

Leo looked up, not realizing he'd been covering his face with his hands. Lillian, Valentina's mother, was staring down at him, her expression barely composed. "How can it not be?"

"You didn't do this. Some sick, sick psycho did. This isn't your fault and you can't afford to lose it now. None of us can. We have to figure this out."

"Figure what out? We don't even know what *this* is. Where do we start looking? Who do we talk to?"

Lillian paused, then sank down onto the couch next to him. "I don't know," she admitted. "I don't know what to do, but we have to do *something*. Just sitting here won't get her back."

Leo knew she was right, though he didn't know where to begin. Work with the police? Put up posters? Drive around looking for suspicious activity?

Never before had he felt so completely lost; for Valentina's sake, he would find his way.

SHE SPENT THE night trembling, desperately trying to stay awake, to protect herself against the suffocating dark. The silence only made it worse, reminding her that she was shut away from the rest of world, left to the mercy of two men who were two very different kinds of psychopaths.

Valentina had seen enough movies and read enough books to know how it worked. Alan was the devious bad guy who would try to reason with her, encourage her to follow the rules, and when he'd had enough, he'd slice her throat without a second thought. Dane was the obvious bad guy, the one who was aching for a taste of blood, barely restrained by whatever rules "the boss" had put in place. The boss, though, she hadn't yet figured out. If she believed Alan, then he was a man who enjoyed hurting women and clearly disposed of them one right after the other.

And she was next in line.

That thought stayed with her throughout the night, eating away at her confidence, pulling down the mask of steadfast strength she'd been determined to uphold. Alan and Dane had brought her into some sort of twisted human trafficking ring, or so she assumed. Why else would they have taken her for another man, not needing her name beforehand, locking her up and sticking to the rules about not touching her? She was thankful for that rule, but sickened by how easily they had made her part of their sinister trade.

Just one day, she thought bitterly. *Just one day is all it took*.

At some point during the black night she managed to find her way to the toilet, though she didn't bother searching for the sink afterwards. She was already filthy and germy hands were the last of her worries, as was the thought of possibly being watched by the mirror camera. Instead she crawled back to her corner and wrapped the blanket around her shaking shoulders, fingers gripping the fabric almost painfully.

When footsteps sounded above her, she knew morning had finally come. Valentina could have stood, but the dark combined with only a few snatches of sleep made her dizzy. So, she remained in the corner until, whether by miracle or an act of mercy, the light flicked on.

For a moment, she was blind. Bright white light flooded her eyes. Valentina covered her face with the blanket until the door lock sounded, causing her to squint in the harsh light lest she be caught unaware. Through the blurry light she could see Alan in the doorway holding a tray.

"Rise and shine," he greeted, his tone far too cheery. "I brought you breakfast."

Valentina stood on shaky legs, unable to deny the fact that she was starving. She couldn't help the disappointment that crossed her face at the sight of a single piece of toast and single hard-boiled egg.

Alan noted the disappointment as well. "Not good enough for you, your highness?" He set the tray down on the floor inches from his feet. "You eat what I give you. No room service here like I'm sure spoiled little girls like you are used to. Besides, the boss likes his girls bony, so you have a few pounds to lose before we present him to you."

Insult overtook disappointment. "Excuse me?" Valentina crossed her arms, letting the blanket fall to the floor. "Are you calling me *fat*? If I'm so undesirable, then why didn't you take some chick who was *already* bony?"

Alan only chuckled and waved a hand at her. "Don't go thinking you're special or something. The boss doesn't care who you are or where you come from. He only cares how you look when he gets here. I'll make sure you're nice and pretty for him."

Before she could reply, he disappeared behind the door. Valentina stared at the closed door incredulously, still insulted. She wasn't bone-thin by any stretch of the imagination, but she certainly wasn't overweight. Her bi-weekly trips to the gym made sure of that. Her body was tone, tough. Hell if she was going to starve herself to please some psycho.

With that in mind, she begrudgingly made her way to the food and ate it all in less than a minute, washing it down with the last of her water. She really was hungry, and that little bit was better than nothing at all. After eating, she sat down on the mattress and contemplated what to do next. The quiet was back, but at least the light was still on. She was exhausted from her all-night terror fest, but the thought of sleeping frightened her even more. Who knew what they would do to her when she eventually drifted out of consciousness.

To take her mind off sleep, Valentina leaned back against the wall and focused on anything, everything, else. She wondered if MoMo was safe, if Leo came home and found evidence of the attack, if her mother had been informed and if so, how she was taking the news.

Since her father's death, it had been just the two of them, Valentina and Lillian against the world. Her father was killed when she was just a child, but her mother had kept his memory alive, always talking about his dedication to the church, willingness to help others, and charming demeanor. Valentina supposed she must take after her mother, then, since she never went to church, rarely volunteered, and wasn't known for being charming. And yet, she still felt connected to her father because, at the very least, she remembered how she felt when she was with him

– comfortable, loved, happy. Many a night was spent sitting on his knee as he read her a book, or dancing to his favorite jazz music, or even putting together a puzzle featuring cartoon characters or nature scenes.

She held on to those memories the most, even after the nightmares started, to remind her of everything her family lost. The sound of her father's voice kept her going during her mother's dark days, during her own night terrors that her shrink would later attribute to the scumbag who'd senselessly taken his life. One of her favorite memories was of her first soccer game as a child.

As the youngest and smallest player on the team, Valentina often felt like the weakest member. She went to every practice and did her best, but on the day of the first game, she wouldn't leave the safety of her mom's SUV. Her father had climbed into the backseat with her, and they sat silently for a few moments before Valentina finally spoke up.

"I'm not as good as them," she had admitted, shuffling her cleat-covered feet. "I'm scared I'm gonna mess up and everyone will be mad at me and laugh at me."

Her father had ruffled her hair, smiling softly. "Fear is fleeting," he'd replied. "It only has power if you believe it does. Be strong. Be confident. Trust in yourself, and fear will fade away, and courage will take its place."

Even though she hadn't fully understood her father that day, his words gave her the courage to play that first game. A couple years later, her mother repeated those same words during his eulogy, reminding everyone in attendance of the brave and kind man he was. Valentina couldn't count the number of times her mother had whispered, "Be strong. Be confident. Fear will fade away," while holding her in a bear hug after a nightmare with The Midnight Man. The words had become their own personal mantra, one that bonded them together and kept alive the memory of a man taken too soon.

She had to get out, if not for herself than for her mother. Losing her daughter as well as her husband would break Lillian, of that much Valentina was sure. She was also sure that she had only herself to count on. There was no way Leo or the police would ever find her. She was too well hidden, and these guys were smart, even though they didn't look or sound it. They knew how to cover their tracks.

No, if she wanted to live through this and escape before the boss came for her, then she needed a plan.

LEO SAT AT the small breakfast table, staring at the newspaper, oblivious to the three people who'd joined him in the kitchen. Just that morning news broke of the kidnapping, in part thanks to his own diligence since he felt like the police weren't yet treating the case like a true missing persons. He'd used his contact at the local paper to get the story and Valentina's picture on the front page, detailing the attack and asking the public for help. He could only hope that the right person, or people, saw the article.

During the brief interview with his friend, Leo made sure to highlight the fact that they found blood and torn jewelry, indicating a physical scuffle. He also insisted they include the exact times she was last seen, and when the discovery of her disappearance had been made, hoping that the timeframe would trigger a memory in a reader. If nothing else, Leo was a writer who understood the importance of giving all the right details.

The article also mentioned a reward for anyone who provided a tip that actually got Valentina back. He expected to get random phone calls from people offering up useless bits of information for the promise of cash, but he had no problem telling them to shove off. No, his money was for the people who truly wanted to and actually could help. That was his task for the day – determining how much he could put toward the reward without losing everything else in his life.

Though he'd give it all up in a heartbeat if it meant seeing Valentina again.

"We have three thousand in savings," he admitted to Lillian, who sat across from him. "We just used a good chunk to remodel her shop and for a trip to California next summer. I'll see if I can get any of that trip refunded and maybe have another grand."

"I have two thousand I can contribute," Lillian offered. "I'll give everything I have to get my daughter back. If I need to sell the TV and car to get more, then I'll do it."

Leo knew she didn't have much, and that two grand was more than she should have been contributing. Still, he reached over and took her hand to comfort her.

"Count us in for nine K," Dom put in from his place leaning against the counter.

Leo turned, disbelief in his eyes. "You have that much you could give up?"

"I save my tips, Dom just got a raise." Slim shrugged, her eyes red from tears and lack of sleep. "And it's Valentina." She pushed off the counter and offered Leo a hug. "We'll do whatever we have to do to get her back."

Leo knew her words were earnest. The four had been close friends for nearly seven years. Valentina and Slim met at the nightclub where Slim bartended, striking up a conversation while drinks were being made that resulted in a lunch planned for the next day. The two had a lot in common yet were complete opposites, which may have been why their friendship worked so well. Where Valentina was quiet, Slim made her opinion known. Where Slim was cautious, Valentina preferred to leap without thinking.

Dom and Leo bonded over a mutual love of football

and home-brewed beer. Before long the four were inseparable, even after kids entered the picture. Leo couldn't imagine life without either one of them, and needed them now more than ever.

A knock sounded at the front door, causing them all to jump. The house had been quiet since the police finally left, none of them speaking hardly above a whisper and rarely a full sentence at that. It was as though Valentina's lack of presence had taken on a form of its own, casting them into silence.

The chair scraped against the tile floor as Leo rose and shuffled to the door. Irritation flashed across his weary face when he opened it to see reporters on the front porch. One of them, a tall, thin, and artificially blond woman, stepped forward.

Before she could ask whatever inane question he was sure was about to leave those red-painted lips, Leo cut her off. "All you need to know is that my wife, Valentina Murdoch, was kidnapped from our home two days ago. Someone took her from this very house, beat her, and abducted her. We don't know where she is or who took her, but we're doing everything in our power to find out. In fact," he did a quick tally in his head, "anyone who offers information that leads to Valentina's whereabouts will get a fourteen-thousand-dollar reward, cash."

A barrage of questions followed his statement, but he had already closed the door. Leo leaned against it, listening to their shouts, refusing to budge. He said what he needed to say, and hoped that people were listening.

Chapter Six

THE DOOR TO her prison squeaked open. Valentina jumped to her feet from the bed, where she'd been dozing in and out despite her earlier resolve to stay awake. Dane entered, wearing the same faded and ragged clothes she first saw him in. Any and all sleepiness instantly melted away when she saw the ropes in his hands.

"Arms behind you, sweets," he ordered.

"Why?"

"'Cuz I'm the one with the knife, that's why."

When Valentina didn't move, Dane walked over and grabbed her by the arm, spinning her around then shoving her against the wall. "Fine," he breathed into her ear, "we'll do it the hard way."

Valentina bit back a grimace as he roped her wrists and forearms at her back, his knees painfully shoved into her thighs to prevent her from moving. When he was finished, he shoved a rough bag that reeked of dead fish over her head and yanked her by the ropes, dragging her across the room and through the door.

Step by step he shoved her to the first floor, barking out insults whenever she tripped and slammed her knees into the wood. Her breath was hot against the sack, coming out in ragged gasps the more she tripped and bumped into walls. Not having her hands free only made her movements that much worse.

Finally, they reached the landing. She guessed by the direction Dane turned her that they were moving away from the front door, which made her heart sink. During her time in the room she'd tried to memorize the lay of the house as best she knew it. This was a new direction, and she had no idea where it would lead.

Something close to hope filled her when she felt a change in the air against her bare arms and she knew she was outside. Outside. Escape. Freedom in the woods. She was so close, she could literally smell it – the scent of grass and dirt and sunshine even through the bag's dead fish odor.

Dane tugged the sack off her head and her eyes watered in the light, but only for a moment. Valentina blinked back the tears and looked around, seeing that she was standing in the middle of a fenced yard. Tall wooden posts surrounded the perimeter, each topped with barb-wire, with no gateway leading to the front.

"You wouldn't even make it to the fence," Dane warned when he caught sight of her peering up at the posts. He stepped back, hands on his hips. "You got one hour."

"One hour for what?"

"The boss don't like his women crazy. Says they gotta go outside once a day to keep their sanity. So ya got one hour."

As much as she hated the reason, Valentina had to admit Dane was right. Being outside *was* good for her health, both mental and physical. Nature was her therapy, a love that originally brought her and Leo together, as they met on a local hiking trail when they happened to be sharing the same lake area for their picnic lunch. They still went hiking and camping often, and enjoyed nights under the stars whenever possible.

So she enjoyed being outside while she could, walking

to the center of the large yard and taking a seat on the grass, stretching her legs out for comfort as best she could with her arms behind her back. The position was awkward, but the sun on her face and the stretch in her muscles felt great. She didn't even care that Dane was watching, or that she was covered in days'-old grime.

While she sat, she devised a plan. There was no way she could scale the fence – and even if she could, the wire would slice her to pieces. That left her escape through the house. She'd seen it already from the front, and now she was able to take in the back. Again, she was surprised by how large it was. The windows were mostly boarded up rather than shuttered. She wondered how many of those rooms were used to house women like herself, or if there were any other captives there at all.

"Just you this time, sweetheart," Dane said from his spot on the back patio. He watched her from the rickety chair, beer in one hand and knife in the other.

Valentina frowned, annoyed that he always knew what she was thinking. She vowed to stop looking at whatever she was contemplating in hopes that she could eventually outsmart the surprisingly astute kidnapper. "This time?" she repeated. "What happened to the others?"

"Boss used 'em up." The answer was so flippant that it caused her stomach to clutch.

"What do you mean?"

"I mean what I said. Boss used 'em up. We got ourselves a good business here, supply and demand as he sees fit. Some of 'em he keeps, some get sold to others."

The pieces fell into place at that, confirming her earlier suspicions. "Your boss is a human trafficker."

Dane tipped his beer at her. "Now you're catching on."

"Then why hasn't he come for me yet?"

"Boss is a busy man, got other places to be. He'll get to ya, don't you worry. We got ya a little early, couldn't pass up the perfect opportunity to snatch ya right outta your house like that."

She wondered why he was taking credit when he wasn't even there, but decided not to ask. She also wasn't going to ask for information she didn't need to know, but did want to keep him talking. "When will he be here?"

Dane lifted a shoulder. "Whenever he wants to be. He don't like to be predictable. Might be tomorrow, might be two weeks. Man's got a business to run."

"Wouldn't good business be not sitting on the goods for too long?"

Dane scoffed. "You ain't gonna spoil, don't you worry. Besides, the boss has got his girls all over to tend to. Gotta settle business with them, then we get to show ya off."

So, she pondered, she didn't have much time. Valentina wouldn't pretend to understand how the business worked, but she got enough from Dane to know that however it all went down, it was fluid. The boss likely had many more houses like this, if not throughout the state then throughout the country or perhaps even the world. Who knew how far their scope went? One thing she knew for sure – she was nothing more than a pawn, an insignificant speck of a larger operation where her only role was to be one person's payday, and another's plaything.

With no way of knowing when the boss would arrive, she had to act fast. The boss wouldn't turn her into a toy, or a statistic.

While she sat on the grass, avoiding Dane's gaze, Valentina envisioned the house. She knew the path from the front door to the basement by memory, and now from the basement to the backyard. The backyard didn't help her due to the fence, but the front door was all she needed. That, and to get the hell away from her captors.

Her plan wasn't quite formulated by the time Dane rose, checking his watch. "Time's up. Get up." Valentina remained sitting, eyeing him closely, face expressionless. "I said up, bitch."

"No thanks, I'm good."

Dane stalked over to her. "So it's gonna be like this?" He reached down and grabbed her by the wrists, jerking her up so hard her shoulders nearly popped out of place. Standing behind her, he reached for the sack in his jacket pocket.

And that's when Valentina moved.

Channeling every bit of movie knowledge she'd ever learned, Valentina kicked back and smashed her bare heel down on the top of his sneakered foot. When he yelled out and shifted, she arched backwards and slammed her head into his face, feeling bone crunch. For just a second, his grip loosened and she used the time to push off the grass.

Valentina raced across the yard, thinking despite her fear that she must look like a gimpy chicken with her arms behind her back. She reached the doorway back into the house, already planning the path through the halls to the front – and to freedom.

Her leg collapsed beneath her before she felt the pain.

She hit the patio hard, hip connecting with stone. Her head nearly bounced off the wall before she caught herself and managed to roll onto her back and lift herself enough to glance down. Only then did she notice why she fell – and the pain racing through her left shin.

Her leg was sliced through the back, a clean cut that exposed blood and tissue beneath her thin pants. The cause of the wound lay a few feet away – Dane's knife, which he had thrown with precision aim, despite his obviously broken nose. He stalked toward her, murder in his bruising eyes, kicking the blade away from her outstretched bound hands.

He slapped her, one hard hit on each cheek. "Don't worry, it won't leave a mark," he sneered down at her. "But this sure as shit will."

Valentina nearly blacked out when his fist connected with her gut once, then twice. Her lungs shuddered, unable to take in air, and her stomach recoiled with bitter bile.

But Dane wasn't done. "Hurts like a bitch, don't it?" he mocked. He stood and kicked her hard in the back, his foot connecting with kidney. He had reared back for a second time when a voice shouted out from inside.

"Enough! If you kill her, the boss'll be after both of us!"

His foot hovered over Valentina's face, which was stained with tears. Finally Dane lowered his leg and took a few steps back, far enough to retrieve his knife. He pointed at her with the blade. "Get the bitch back to her room before I slice her open."

Alan half carried, half dragged Valentina back to the room after covering her face, an act she now found completely ridiculous. Even if she could see, she couldn't even walk, and likely wouldn't be able to for at least the next few days. They made it back to the basement prison after several bumps into the walls that resulted in her landing in a pile at the bottom of the stairs. Every part of her felt broken as Alan brought her into the room and left, only to return a moment later with a first aid kit.

"It's your own fault," he told her plainly, directing her to the mattress and keeping her bloody leg over the floor. With expert movements, he cut off her pants at the knee and began to roughly, but efficiently, clean the wound. Valentina grit her teeth together at the first sting, wishing she could ask him to be gentler, knowing the request would be futile. "When you misbehave, you get punished."

She wanted to respond, but her jaw was clenched, as were her fists. Valentina could only endure the pain as her captor cleaned the wound, then placed several bandages with gauze over it. "No stitches," he explained. "Unless, of course, you want me to attempt to sew you up." He laughed at the panic in her eyes, then wrapped her leg in medical tape. "Knife went clean through the muscle, and maybe a tendon. I'm not a doctor, so I can't be sure. I do know that you're going to be in a lot of pain and be wishing you'd followed the rules earlier. Now, keep still or it will open up, and the last thing I need is you bleeding out everywhere."

She didn't move, not even when he turned his back on her to collect the medical supplies. Plenty of visions crossed her mind, ways to strangle him, how to trip him, crawling through the open door and up the stairs. But the truth was, she wasn't sure she could lift a single finger to help herself at the moment. She was at the mercy of the man who'd kidnapped her, and right now, that was all she had going for her.

WHEN NIGHTTIME CAME – or what she assumed to be night by the time the lights went out – Valentina alternated between fear, fogginess, and fury. At first she kept her eyes closed against the dark, but that only made her nauseous. Then she huddled in the corner staring at nothing, but the pain in her leg forced her back to the mattress.

Finally, she managed to get comfortable, but only because her mind couldn't take any more and decided to shut itself down. For hours she lay in the blackness, catching snatches of sleep amidst what she prayed were hallucinations rather than nightmares finally come to life.

She saw him wavering in the night, a blurry vision, the man whose face she sometimes worried she'd forgotten. He spoke to her, his words lost in a silent breeze. Still she listened, remembering the sound of his voice, pretending her father was next to her, comforting her, telling her that she was strong enough to survive this.

Fear will fade away, and courage will take its place.

He disappeared in a swirl of gray, and Leo took his place. The other man in her life, her other love. His back was to her and she could see the tension in his shoulders. She called out to him, telling her husband where she was, what had happened, but he never turned around. Tears filled her eyes as he started to walk off, disappearing into clouded trees. She called out to him, begging him to come back to her, to find her, to take her home and save her from this horrible infested pit, but it was too late. Leo was gone, and she was on her own.

Then a new figure appeared, the shadow blacker than black, the outline of a man wearing a long coat and wide-brimmed hat. She'd never seen his face. Not once in her lifetime of nightmares had he ever allowed her to see just who he was. Sometimes she imagined him to be a cowboy, other times a 1920s bootlegger, and in other dreams an old-timey Englishman. But no matter how she envisioned him, The Midnight Man still haunted her.

And tonight, he laughed at her pain.

The sound filled her, the hoarse tone echoing all around her tiny room. It consumed her until she couldn't move, held down to the mattress by sheer terror. He reached for her, fingers grazing her throat, though she clutched the blanket tightly to her chest to ward off his impending attack. Her lips moved in a silent prayer she didn't believe in, praying for the strength to get through this night, this hour, this minute.

Then the sickness came. Whether from fever or fear or fatigue, Valentina couldn't stop it. She retched violently, gut cramping, eyes watering, arms shaking from holding herself over the grimy toilet. Only when her stomach was empty did she collapse back on the concrete floor, exhausted.

Chapter SEVEN

LEO STRUGGLED TO eat breakfast, forcing himself to take bite after bite. He could barely handle food at this point, but knew he needed to maintain his strength if he was going to find his wife.

He'd spent the past week speaking to various news outlets, working with the police, and walking the property searching for clues. So far, nothing led to Valentina; nothing even came close. Whoever took her was a pro, leaving behind no tracks to follow. Dom and Slim had put up posters around town asking for clues, and Lillian spent her days alternating between crying and taking care of Valentina's business – or as much as she could just to keep the plants from dying. She had to do something, and if she couldn't find her daughter, then she would keep her shop running until she got back.

Working in the shop renewed Lillian's drive, helping to keep her spirits up. So many customers came in to express their condolences, and more to offer their assistance. Valentina was loved by her clientele, not just because of her expertise, but because of who she was as a person. The overwhelming amount of support made Lillian realize how foolish she had been to discourage her daughter to open *Planting Roots*, as Valentina clearly knew what she was doing – and did it well.

Putting his plate in the sink, Leo picked up a stack of posters with Valentina's picture and his contact information. He was going to head a little farther out of town today to put up more posters and ask around town for any possible information.

Leo yanked open the front door, then stopped when he saw a young man on his front porch, hand raised as if to knock. "Can I help you?" he asked, observing the visitor. The man was in his late teens, perhaps early twenties, fit and clean shaven.

"Um, yeah," he replied, lowering his hand. "My name's Jake Hemworth. My sister lives a few streets over. She told me about your wife, and I thought maybe I could come talk to you."

Leo frowned, suspicious but also hopeful. "About what?"

"Well, I might have some information for you."

For a moment, Leo only stared at the man, trying to decide if he was being honest or deceitful. He'd never been a good judge of character, but was learning how to better read people, especially those who truly wanted to help and those who just wanted a chance at the reward money.

Finally, he stepped back and gestured for him to enter. Leo led Jake to the dining room, both taking a seat at the table. "So, what information do you have for me?"

"Well," Jake began, "I came down to visit my sister for about a week when my nephew was having his birthday party. I live down in California, so I haven't seen the family much lately. Anyway, I like to run in the morning, so I'd been taking some different routes each time, just for a change of scenery. I've never been here before, and I like all the nature trails. Anyway, the day your wife was taken, I was jogging past your house."

Leo felt anticipation build, but he stayed silent.

"I was past your driveway, didn't even really stop to

consider if anyone lived down here since you can't see the house from the road. I was toward the end of the street when I heard a car, so I looked over my shoulder to make sure I was out of the way, and moved into the grass. A car was pulling out of your driveway, going pretty fast. I thought it was weird at the time, the speed I mean, but figured whoever it was just had a lead foot."

Leo found his voice. "Did… Do you remember what kind of car it was?"

Jake sighed. "Not really. I hate to admit it, being a guy and all, but I'm not good with car types. I'd probably know if it I saw it. It was dark, really dark blue if not black. Nothing flashy. Four-door car, a little boxy, kinda like something you'd expect to see an old guy driving. Seats looked gray." Jake stared out the window as if trying to remember the day. "The guy driving, I only caught a glance of him. Middle-aged man, looked kind of, I don't know, greasy. Like the used car dealer stereotype. Brown hair, thin. Looked straight ahead the entire time."

Jake leaned back, blew out a breath. "He kept driving on the main road and passed me, going straight until he was out of sight. To be honest, I didn't think anything of it and didn't even really remember by the time I finished my run. I flew out that night and didn't hear about your wife's kidnapping until my sister called and asked if I remembered seeing anything. I wanted to help, so I came back this weekend, thought I could talk to the cops."

A lump formed in Leo's throat, one that he had to swallow back. "You'd tell all this to the police?"

"Of course."

"Thank you." Leo stood and Jake followed. "You have no idea how much this means."

Jake nodded. "I don't know how much it will help, but—"

"Any information is better than none," Leo cut in.

"Right now all we've been doing is praying for a break, and if you're telling the truth, then this could be the break we need."

The younger man ran a hand through his short hair. "I'm sure you've got all kinds of sickos getting their kicks by making shit up, but I swear I'm telling the truth. But, I mean…I wouldn't get your hopes up about something like this."

Leo stared at Jake for a moment, deciding he was being honest. "I appreciate that. And I have reward money, if this leads to Valentina."

"Nah, man, I don't want your money." Jake held up a hand. "Just get your wife back."

A STRANGE, FOREIGN sound woke Valentina from her slumber. Her muscles quivered as she pulled herself to a sitting position, wincing at the pounding headache behind her eyes. She was hungry despite the night of vomiting and her leg protested with each movement, though it surprisingly didn't hurt as badly as the day before.

Leaning against the wall, she listened carefully for the noise again. It sounded almost like crying, or perhaps… screaming, she mused. She'd thought she was alone, and her heart went out to whatever poor soul had been brought to this horror house.

Valentina didn't move when the door opened. She had heard Alan coming – she knew the sound of his footsteps versus Dane's by now – and figured he'd arrive with a bottle of water and a piece of bread. She was surprised to see scrambled eggs and oatmeal added to the plate.

"Don't get used to it, Miss Tina," Alan said as he set the tray by the mattress. "It's just to keep your strength up after losing all that blood."

She glanced down, not at all shocked to see the dried blood on her skin and clothes or the drag marks across the floor. It should have made her sick to see her own blood everywhere, but instead she felt indifferent. For some reason it seemed almost fitting that her small basement cage be covered in her blood. That indifference quickly fizzled out when she heard the sound again – definitely a scream. But not just any scream.

This one came from a child.

Valentina jumped to her feet, shocked by her nimble movements, bracing herself against the wall with a shaking hand. Her eyes were wide, her tone accusing. "You have a kid here?" A little girl, if she had to guess.

Alan only shrugged. "We have a business to run, Miss Tina. I'm sure you understand."

"Dane said it was just me."

"Well, Dane's known to be a bit of a liar."

So, Valentina wondered, had the kid been there all along? "What are you doing to her?"

A knowing smirk crossed his face at the question. "Don't you worry about the little one. We're taking good care of her."

She didn't know how to interpret his response, but something about the glint in his eyes and the way he emphasized *good* told her what she needed to know. Valentina took a step forward, then hesitated when Alan produced a gun from his back. The gun was a sudden shift from the usual knife stuck in her face, and the change made her uneasy.

"Don't do anything stupid now, Miss Tina. Wouldn't want a matching wound, would you?" He backed up and left the room.

Valentina unclenched her jaw long enough to sit down and eat, hoping to refuel her strength, all the while planning exactly how she was going to kill her kidnappers. It was more than personal now. She could handle the hits. She could deal with a knife wound to the leg, and had her own justice in mind for retribution, if she was ever lucky enough to escape. But bringing a child into the house, one who had likely been there longer than Valentina, burned her to the core. They would suffer for what they'd done to her, and even more for the child.

She couldn't help but wonder if there were more kids locked up somewhere in the house, or even other women. If Dane lied about her being the only one, then who knew how many more were suffering the same fate. Briefly, Valentina thought back to the news program she'd been watching the morning of her capture. Two children abducted in broad daylight – one of them may have been the owner of that haunting scream. She couldn't recall hearing of any missing women lately, but if there were any here, Valentina vowed to try her best to save them too.

It was a short while later that Dane came for her.

"Get your clothes," he ordered, nodding toward the pile she'd dumped in the corner.

"Why?"

"'Cuz I said so. And 'cuz you need a bath. You stink."

She couldn't deny that simple fact. It had been days since she'd bathed, and she had started to smell like the stale, moldy room as well as last night's sickness. With a sigh, Valentina lifted herself from the mattress and grabbed the clothes, hissing out a protest when Dane took hold of her arm.

"Be smart, sweetheart. Otherwise I'll cut ya again, this time somewhere a little more…special."

She wasn't interested in being sliced and scarred any more than she already was, so Valentina did as she was told, allowing Dane to shove a thin bag over her head and push her up the stairs. Her leg protested with each step as she limped along, biting back grimaces and bitter retorts to his orders.

Once on the first floor, she realized with some amount of surprise that she could partially see out of the sack covering her face. This one didn't smell as bad as the first one and was thinner, allowing bits of light to pierce through the scratchy material. Her eyes immediately went to one of the windows, which was covered by a thin curtain, allowing sunshine to stream through. She relished the sight, as faded and cloudy as it was, knowing she'd never be allowed back outside after her last stunt.

Dane shoved her forward and she stumbled, catching herself only when her shoulder hit the doorjamb. "Keep walking," he demanded.

"To where?" she asked, not moving. The bag may have been thin, but the hallways were dark and didn't make for easy navigation.

"Bathroom. I told ya, you stink."

Valentina sighed, but had to admit the thought of a shower sounded appealing. She continued to move forward, then paused when she heard voices coming from another room. Just before they entered yet another hall, she peeked around the corner and into what looked like a living room. Two men sat on the sun-faded tan couch. One was Alan, the other she didn't recognize.

"Who's he talking to?" she asked, sketching the man's face in her mind as best she could. Through the thin material, she made out a blurry figure no older than twenty, twenty-one, judging by his youthful face and trendy apparel. He was sitting back on the couch, perfectly at ease with a gun sitting on the armrest while the woman was being shoved through the house.

"Doesn't concern you," Dane answered gruffly, taking hold of her elbow and dragging her into the bathroom, where he removed the bag from her head.

Valentina blinked in the harsh fluorescent light,

surprised by the size of the room. The bathroom was spacious, with a double sink, separate toilet, and a tile shower with glass doors. There were no adornments, no toiletries save for soap, shampoo, conditioner, and a single towel. The coldness of the room annoyed her more than anything, though she had to admit that at this point, she didn't really care.

She turned when she heard the door shut behind her, with Dane on the wrong side. "What are you doing?"

He only pointed to the shower. "Clean up."

Valentina arched a single brow, clutching the clothes to her chest. "I am *not* taking a shower with you in here."

"You will, or I'll slice you open again."

They both stood their ground for a moment, Dane with his arms crossed and feet firmly planted in front of the door, Valentina in front of the shower half turned away from him. She wondered how to get out of having to shower, but also hated the idea of going back to the room filthy. Pride, dignity, and frustration warred within her until she realized that a refusal was exactly what Dane was hoping for, since that would give him another excuse to hurt her.

Finally, Valentina broke the stare and purposely strode to the shower with a heavy limp. She set the clothes down on a small stool next to the shower and reached behind her, unsnapping her bra. They had only given her pants, a shirt, and underwear to change into, and hell if she was going braless around them after getting clean. But she also didn't want to get it wet, like she planned to do with her other clothes.

Two could play at this game.

Her eyes never left Dane's as she pulled one arm out of the bra strap, then the other, tossing the item onto the pile of clean clothes. She saw him swallow and shift slightly, eyes darkening. It almost amused her that he thought he'd be getting a show, and she held on to that feeling since it was better than the alternative – sickening herself with the thought of him seeing her naked. Regardless, she knew he wouldn't like what she did next.

Valentina turned on the shower and waited for hot water, then stepped in, fully clothed.

"What the fuck you doing?"

"Taking a shower."

"You can't shower with your clothes on."

"Watch me."

Dane stepped forward, hands in fists. "Maybe I'll cut them off you."

Valentina faced him, water soaking into her hair and clothes. "Maybe I'll tell the boss you put your hands all over me." She saw the threat register and was thankful Dane was more afraid of this so-called boss than he was interested in pursuing whatever disgusting thoughts were being entertained in his head.

When he relented, leaning back against the counter with a grunt, she stepped beneath the spray of water, enjoying every moment of the warmth despite the situation. She wetted herself down even in clothes, keeping her body half turned from Dane, who was watching her intently. It seemed odd to her that he would be the one tasked with babysitting her while she showered, given their previous history.

Despite herself, she had to ask. "Why are you here and not Alan?"

Dane shifted against the sink, eyes never leaving her. He watched her run soap up and down her arms. "He ain't got no interest."

"In what?"

He sneered. "Let's just say he likes 'em young. Me, I like a woman with a little…experience."

She fought the shudder that worked its way up

her back and struggled to maintain a calm expression. "Charming."

Refusing to let the truth register of what Dane just told her, Valentina turned her eyes to the red-tinted water, watching blood wash down the drain. So much of it streamed down from her body without her needing to do anything that she wondered if she had open wounds somewhere other than her leg. Surely this wasn't normal.

Carefully, she lifted each pants leg and washed as high up as she could, gingerly moving around the soiled bandage. She did the same with the rest of her body, never letting Dane see what he wanted to see, even if that meant she couldn't clean every part of herself. Then she moved to her hair, washing away the dirt and sweat and blood. She'd never been a vain person, but knowing her hair was clean made her feel more human and, strangely, like she had a better shot of surviving.

Heroes only survive if they're pretty.

The thought almost made her smile, especially since she knew it was true according to Hollywood. She'd make herself as pretty as she had to be if it meant going home.

When she was finished, Valentina wrung out her clothes as best she could without removing them and used the towel for the rest of her body. She put the bra on first, then pulled the clean shirt on over the wet one, dressing without showing off too much skin, much to Dane's disapproval. The bottoms were trickier, but after wrapping the towel around her waist, she managed to wiggle out of the old pants and into the new.

Valentina resisted smirking when she finished dressing, not even caring that her clean clothes were a bit damp from her awkward dressing attempt. She was surprised Dane didn't take the towel away to yet again prove how much of a prick he was, but supposed her earlier threat had him hesitant. However, he wasted no time in shoving the sack over her head, hauling her out of the bathroom, and pushing her back toward the basement.

Her leg screamed in pain, immediately halting any plans she may have been considering to make a run for it. Still, she couldn't help but think about it. Shove Dane away, run for the window, the door, anywhere. Fight tooth and nail to get her ass out of there and into the woods. There, she could hide, wait for nighttime, make her way to town by moonlight. She could be free.

There is a child here.

Valentina couldn't get that fact out of her mind. There was a child here, somewhere upstairs, and that child was being hurt, tortured even, at the hands of a man who "liked 'em young." She may not have wanted kids, or even liked them all that much, but she couldn't bear the thought of that.

She struggled to remember the name spoken on the news. A little girl taken right out from under her mother… Ally Jameson, Valentina recalled. And there was another missing as well, a little boy… Sam? She wondered if both were here, or if something worse had already happened to the boy.

The names rang through her head as Dane pushed her through the house. Something kept her from speaking them aloud or asking questions. Instead, she thought it prudent to keep her thoughts to herself and rethink her escape plan.

As they passed the living room, Valentina snuck another glance, seeing the same baby-faced man still sitting on the couch. He glanced up as they passed, then lowered his eyes with the slightest shake of his head – a sad shake, she noted, nearly regretful. That interested her, though she wasn't sure what to make of it.

"You keep up those looks, I'll put on a blindfold next time," Dane warned, gripping her shoulder hard enough to bruise.

"Well, who is he?"

"Shut up."

Valentina pressed her lips together when his fingers dug in deeper and kept her mouth shut until she was alone in her room, the door once again locked behind her.

Chapter Eight

SHE WAS STARTING to relish the time alone, not having to worry about being hit or shoved. Now that she was clean, not knowing how long that would last, Valentina stood in front of the mirror, observing her wounds. Her face was starting to heal from her initial beating, the ugly purple bruises fading to yellow and the swelling somewhat reduced around her eye. But, she realized as she pulled down her shirt collar, she now had new marks, bruises in the shape of fingers.

Knowing she was being watched by the camera in the corner, Valentina turned her back to the wall and pulled up her shirt slightly, enough to see what other marks covered her body. She could see exactly where she'd been kicked, punched, shoved. Her skin was a canvas of abuse and she couldn't do a damn thing about it.

Or could she?

She may have been a prisoner, but goddamn it, she wasn't helpless. Valentina struggled to remember everything, anything, she'd ever seen in a movie or TV show. What did captives do?

They cry. And are generally annoying.

Her lips turned upward in a wry grin. She didn't want to be the annoying heroine. She wanted to be the one who kicked ass. What about them?

They observe. They adjust.

Adjusting meant teaching herself how to depend solely on what was available. And most importantly, to never give up hope that she would get the hell out.

She could do that. She *would* do that. Something had sparked within her at hearing the child's scream, strengthening the fight within her, the drive for survival.

So, she would survive.

HOURS AFTER JAKE left the police station, Leo met with the officers. It had been a frustrating day, but, he hoped, also a rewarding one.

The police spent hours working with Jake, questioning him over and over again. His story stayed the same, with no new details. Once they were satisfied he was telling the truth, they began searching for the car, showing the young man model after model until, finally, he pointed to one that matched the getaway vehicle. Though he wasn't sure on the color, he insisted it was either dark blue or black. Either way, it gave the police something to work with. After determining the vehicle, Jake met with the sketch artist, giving as many details as he could remember until they had a picture he felt best reflected his memory.

Now, Leo sat at a desk staring at the picture. Across from him, Sheriff Barnes spoke with another department on the phone. When he finally hung up, Leo had turned away from the image, disgusted with the sleazy smirk and beady eyes that stared up at him.

"We're running the image through the database now," Barnes told Leo, moving the picture away from the distraught husband. "If this guy is a match for anyone in the system, then we'll find him."

Leo doubted that, as he didn't see how any match

could be made with just a sketch, no matter how advanced the technology. But he didn't voice his doubts. Instead he scrubbed his hands over his face and sighed. "What about the car?"

"We can put an alert out for the make, model, and color, let locals know what to be on the lookout for. We'll match it with the sketch. I know it seems like a long shot, but you'd be surprised by how many people are willing to help. People watch the news. They want to catch these guys just as much as we do."

"That may be, but…so what?" Leo watched the news too. He knew how many men, women, and children went missing, only to have their bodies found in a field or behind a dumpster. "Their intentions might be good, but what are the chances of actually finding Valentina?"

Barnes observed Leo, noting the heavy shadows on his face and the slump in his shoulders. This was a man in constant grief, but also one who refused to give up. "There is always a chance," he finally replied. "I don't stop until I find them. I haven't given up on the children, and I won't give up on Valentina."

Leo lifted his eyes to meet the sheriff's. "The children? Do you think there is a connection?"

"There's a chance," Barnes admitted. "It's something we're considering and working on connecting. If we can figure out who this guy is," he tapped the sketch, "then we have a much better shot of figuring out exactly what we're dealing with."

It didn't matter much to Leo if the kidnappings were connected, unless finding the kids meant finding his wife. He stood from the hard, wooden chair and nodded. "Well then, let's put together the pieces."

Chapter NINE

SITTING ON THE mattress, her good leg pulled up against her chest and her chin resting on her knee, Valentina thought.

She thought about the room, what parts of the house she'd seen. She thought about the house from the outside, all the windows. Four stories at least, with an attic and basement. Shitty furniture, but sturdy doors and locks. Lots of narrow hallways that twisted and turned, opening up into side rooms with boarded-up windows.

She thought about the little girl, Ally Jameson. If the news report was right, then she'd been here for weeks, a month even, assuming Valentina's calculations of her own capture were correct. Why she was still here, and what they were doing to her, were considerations too dark to ponder for long.

She thought about her captors, the ones she knew of. Alan, with his sleazy fake charm, who liked 'em young. Dane, who got off on violence and made no secret of his lustful desires. The boss, the unseen threat, the one who would be coming for her soon. And finally, the unnamed man whose role in all this was yet to be discovered. All of them were the enemy, and if given the chance, she would spare them no mercy.

Valentina didn't consider herself to be tough or even

the least bit violent. She was the child who took care of the injured baby birds, the teenager who never said anything mean about anyone else, the adult who stayed focused on her career and future. She prided herself on being able to stay calm and think through situations rather than act rashly.

But this was different. This wasn't caring for sick animals or being a good friend or opening a business. This was a real-life kidnapping, with Valentina as the star of her own horror story. She couldn't afford to find the solution that worked best for everyone, only for herself. She didn't have the luxury of time. Getting out of here meant being someone entirely different from herself – the hero of all the movies she loved so much.

When the light over her head went out, Valentina fought the shiver that threatened her entire body.

"Okay," she whispered to herself, staring straight ahead at nothing, "first things first."

She was useless if she was afraid. Valentina knew that. And the first way to stop being afraid was to conquer her biggest fear.

Fear will fade away, and courage will take its place.

Her shoulders shook so hard that her neck tensed up, but Valentina refused to close her eyes. If she was going to be brave, be the hero of her own story, then she had to face her fears of The Midnight Man. She'd tried this dozens of times over the years and failed miserably each time, always retreating back to the nightlight for comfort and salvation.

In her mind's eye she saw him, the shadowy trench coat blowing in the wind, wide-brimmed hat silhouetted against the moonlight. She imagined him getting closer, something silver flashing at his belt. A gun – perhaps a knife.

Her heart beat wildly, hands clenching into fists. Valentina struggled to breathe evenly, barely blinking, her back pressed up against the paneling as though trying to disappear into it. Hide, blend in with the darkness, fade away into nothing so no one could see or hurt her.

Still he kept coming, hand moving to the silver at his waist. He would reach her, and he would kill her.

Unless she stopped him first.

"Stay away from me," Valentina whispered, eyes trained on a figure in the darkness that only she could see. In some part of her mind, she knew no one was there, but knowing that didn't take away the fear of a nightmare that had plagued her since childhood. She'd tried so many times to conquer her demons, only to fall victim night after night.

But this time was different. This time, her life was at stake – as well as that of a child. She wasn't fighting just for a good night's sleep. This was survival, and hell if she wasn't going to be the fittest.

"I'm not afraid of you," she whispered, not sure if she was convincing The Midnight Man…or herself. "I'm not afraid of you. I'm not afraid of you. I'm not afraid of you." She didn't care if anyone was watching her from the camera, or if she sounded insane. She repeated the statement over and over again until she finally began to believe it.

And to prove it, she shifted and lay down on the dirty mattress, then closed her eyes and attempted to sleep.

I'm not afraid of you.

At first, panic started to set in, but still she told herself that her mind was more powerful than her fear.

I'm not afraid of you.

Soon her sweaty palms began to dry and her shoulders stopped shaking.

I'm not afraid of you.

Though she couldn't get the image of the shadowy man completely out of her thoughts, Valentina finally drifted off to sleep.

SHE AWOKE LONG before her breakfast was delivered. Valentina was getting better at snapping awake when she needed to, never being caught unaware. It was easier to shake the sleep from her mind and limbs today, considering she actually managed to rest the night before.

It hadn't been easy, but after hours of repeating her new personal mantra, she'd fallen into a deep sleep. Twice the nightmares came, but not as strong as in the past – and only one had frightened her enough to jar her awake. While she couldn't say that her sleep had been pleasant or restful, Valentina did feel more refreshed than she had been since being brought to the house.

Rising to a sitting position, she glanced around and realized why she had been pulled from slumber – the light was on. Before anyone entered, Valentina pulled up the baggy pants leg and observed her leg. The swelling had gone down some, but the skin around the wound was red and still painful to the touch. The jagged edges of the cut itself were scabbed over and disgusting enough that Valentina averted her eyes. She hoped Alan would bring the first aid kit again so she could at least change the bandage.

As if on cue, the door to the basement opened and then, just moments later, he appeared in her room holding a tray. She saw food, a bottle of water, and fresh bandages. Valentina accepted the food wordlessly and stuck out her leg when he gestured.

"Looks better," Alan commented after removing the old wrappings. "I take it you learned your lesson?"

She didn't answer, for she knew that if she spoke, she would unleash the rage stirring within her at what he'd done to that little girl.

"Feeling any pain?" Again, Valentina ignored him. "I could give you something for the pain, if you want."

Alan sat back on his heels and observed her for a moment before cleaning the wound. "You know," he said casually, eyes trained on her leg as he wrapped the bandage around, "your husband is a real piece of work." He lifted a brow when Valentina sat up straighter. "Oh, that caught your attention, did it, Miss Tina?"

He paused, then continued. "Couldn't help but catch the news last night. As it turns out, some jogger saw us leaving that morning. Got us narrowed down to a car type and color, and even a nice little sketch of the driver."

His casual tone turned icy. "But don't you worry, Miss Tina. They won't find us here. We've got you nice and tucked away. But I must say, if your husband doesn't shut his mouth, Dane just might have to go pay him a visit."

Her words caught in her throat at the threat, and Alan only chuckled at her silence. "Have a good day, Miss Tina."

Emotions battled within her. Valentina ate the toast and egg with tears burning in the corners of her eyes. She didn't want to believe what Alan told her. Or rather, she only wanted to believe part of it. Leo was looking for her, and making ground. Of course he was. She knew he wouldn't rest until he had answers, until she was safe in his arms. And if Alan was telling the truth, he was getting closer.

But at what cost? That was the part she didn't want to believe. She knew what Dane was willing to do, what they both would do to protect their operation. Would Leo lose his life for trying to save hers?

Not if she had any say in it.

Be strong.

Her father had always meant strength in character, but in this case, she was going to apply it to her physical self.

Valentina knew she was weak. They fed her enough to keep her alive and not much more. She could feel the muscles she'd worked hard to tone slowly fading, her body shutting down, her limbs stiffening. With each day and night that passed, her body suffered.

So do something about it.

With renewed spirit, Valentina stretched out her
legs and leaned over, reaching for her toes. It felt good
to stretch, something she didn't do often enough, which
was why she often felt sore after workouts. She tried to
remember what she'd learned at the gym about proper
technique, though it was difficult to move with her injured
leg and bruised body.

Once her legs felt limber, she stood and stretched her
back, arms, shoulders, and neck, keeping her gaze straight
ahead or on the floor instead of the not-so-hidden mirror.
She wondered if Alan or Dane was watching, and if they
were curious as to what she was doing.

An idea occurred to her, and she turned to the bed,
taking the blanket off the mattress. She hobbled over to
the corner and stared up at the two-way mirror. In the
reflection, she could see how battered and exhausted she
looked, but hidden beneath all that, she also saw someone
else – a fighter, a woman who was ready to kick some ass.

The mirror was high, so high that she couldn't touch
the bottom with even her fingertips when standing on her
toes. It took her a few tries, but finally she got the blanket
snagged on the mirror so that it covered almost the entire
thing. Valentina smiled to herself, then got back to the
floor. She wanted to exercise, gain some strength back, but
didn't want *them* watching her.

She started with pushups, having to stop around twenty
to take a break, then did twenty more. Next she attempted
crunches, but the concrete floor hurt her back, so she
moved to the mattress for padding. Leg lifts were next, and
by the end of those she had worked up a good sweat and
finished off her water from breakfast.

She'd just finished her workout when she heard
footsteps on the stairs. Alan and Dane burst into the room,
Dane pointing a gun at her chest in a silent threat. Alan

ignored her and stalked to the mirror, snatching the blanket down and bundling it to his chest. Just as quickly as they came, they disappeared, taking the blanket with them.

Valentina glanced around the room. *Well, that backfired,* she thought, annoyed that she'd have to sleep without any sort of cover. Then, despite herself, she grinned. The workout felt good, gave her energy even though she was tired. More importantly, it renewed her spirit and gave her the confidence boost she needed in this time of darkness.

Chapter TEN

THE POLICE STATION was abuzz with activity when Leo hurried in, eager to speak with the sheriff. Barnes met him in the lobby and led him back to his office, gesturing for the other man to take a seat.

"So, what is it? Do you have a lead?" Leo asked as he sat. His eyes were hopeful, though he told himself not to get too excited.

"We have more than a lead," Barnes replied. "We have a name." He took a seat behind his desk and tapped a few keys on the keyboard. An image popped up on the computer screen. "We got a call yesterday from a woman who saw the sketch on the news. She said he resembled a guy she used to know when she worked at a bar a few towns over. Said he was a regular there. Anyway, we ran his name, and sure enough, he fits the sketch."

Leo leaned over, eager to see the comparison. His stomach turned at the sight of the man, and he realized that Jake had been right when he compared him to the sleazy used car salesman stereotype. The man's eyes were watery and...*just plain slimy*, Leo thought. He was smirking in his mugshot, his expression suggesting how little he thought of his future incarceration.

"His name is Alan Fredericks," Barnes informed Leo. "He was arrested back in ninety-nine for abduction in

Massachusetts, got off on a technicality during his trial. At the time he was suspected of being involved with a trafficking ring, though it was never proven. He dropped off the face of the planet after getting off."

"Seems he found his way back," Leo murmured, knowing in his gut that this was the guy. He supposed he may have just *wanted* this to be the guy, since that would mean they were that much closer to finding Valentina, but there were too many similarities to think otherwise. A criminal who dropped off the face of the earth after being arrested for abduction, a possible tie with a trafficking ring, a guy who just plain looked like a sleazeball – Alan Fredericks had to be the one they were searching for.

And yet, another part of him really hoped he was wrong. If Alan Fredericks was the one who had taken Valentina, then his wife may be facing much more than a kidnapping. Leo knew enough about trafficking to know one important fact – his wife could be sold off to the highest bidder, and never be found. The thought nearly made him sick.

"So what do we do now?"

Barnes sat back, drumming his fingers on the desk. Just outside his office, deputies were already starting the search for one Alan Fredericks. "Now, we list him officially as a suspect. Let people know we're looking for him, and hopefully, someone comes forward. Or, that he screws up. He screwed up the first time by letting the jogger see him, so it's only a matter of time until he does so again."

Leo didn't like the sound of that. "Yeah, but how long could that be? Valentina could be dead by that time, or sold off to some sick fuck who gets off on buying women. We need to get her now. Can't you, I don't know, go question his friends or something?"

"He has no known associates," Barnes answered, frustration clear in his voice. "That's the thing about this guy. He's slick, and he's professional. But don't you worry, Mr. Murdoch. We're getting closer."

DESPITE HER SORE limbs, Valentina continued to exercise, taking breaks when her leg wouldn't allow her to stand any longer, or when nightfall came and had her fighting shivers and hallucinations until the light graced her again. Three days passed, and though they weren't many, they were filled with enough adrenaline-pumping exercise to renew Valentina's energy. Nights were the hardest, pushing herself to stare into the darkness, forcing away images of haunting shadows and sounds of gunfire that still haunted her dreams. She slept only as much as she needed to, always keeping an eye and ear out for any chance at escape.

So far, they hadn't let her leave the room again, not even for another shower. Valentina could certainly smell herself, but knew that if she asked, they wouldn't let her bathe just out of spite. She did, however, hear another child's cry. This one was a little bit lower, a boy's voice, which confirmed that both Ally and Samuel were somewhere in the house. She wanted to help them, almost as much as she wanted to help herself. She felt guilty for thinking of her own desire for escape above theirs, but supposed that was simply survival instinct, since she certainly had no motherly instinct within her.

Still, hearing the child's cry and knowing there were two kids trapped somewhere in the house kept Valentina moving. By her calculations she'd only been at her workout attempts for a few days, but those hours were enough to reenergize her beaten body.

On the fourth morning of her newly implemented exercise regime, that all changed.

Alan entered first, Dane at his heels holding a chair in

one hand and a gun in the other. Valentina pressed herself against the back wall, then snarled when Dane set down the chair and reached for her. Her fight was useless, as he merely spun her around and twisted her arm behind her back, threatening to break her wrist lest she settle down.

Satisfied that she wasn't going to struggle further, the men forced her into the chair, which was facing the mirror and sink, putting her back to the door. Dane came into view, holding the gun steady with her forehead, so close she swore she could see straight up the barrel.

No, was all she could think as Alan bound her arms behind her at the wrist and her ankles to the chair legs. The loaded gun kept her from moving, but after Alan stepped away, she fought the restraints, though her efforts did little more than cause her skin to chafe.

"We know what you've been doing, Miss Tina," Alan said, coming into view. "We can't allow that. So now you get to sit here and think about what you've done."

"Let me go," she demanded, hating how pathetic the command sounded. "You want me to stop, I'll stop. Just untie me."

"Fat chance, sweets." Dane smacked her in the back of the head with the gun, laughing when she winced. "You ain't exactly proved trustworthy in the past. You're more trouble than you're worth, ya know? The boss'll have fun breaking this one," he added to Alan as the two left the room.

Alone, Valentina stared at herself in the mirror, only able to see her head, shoulders, and chest. She didn't like what stared back at her – a woman with shadowed eyes, listless expression, and knotted hair. Any energy she may have felt from her few days of exercise had fled, leaving her body depleted and languid.

Well, you really pissed them off this time.

She didn't think a few pushups and stretches would

make them worry. Apparently being optimistic about escape was a big no-no in the kidnapper world. Valentina guessed they truly did want her broken and depressed, easily molded to the boss's will when the time came.

Well, fuck, she thought, half-heartedly pulling at the ropes before accepting that the knots were never going to budge. Her fingers worked at them anyway, just for some false sense of hope.

It would take more than this to break her, even though they left her there all day, unable to move, unable to escape. Boredom more than anything else threatened to drive her insane, hours upon hours of staring at the same wall in the same position with the same dark thoughts traveling her mind.

Valentina had never been one to sit for long and preferred being active, so she attempted to keep herself entertained by singing her favorite songs in her head and playing her favorite movie scenes in her mind.

She was almost relieved when the door opened again.

For a moment she heard only shuffling, then Alan came into view holding a bowl and spoon. He leaned against the sink. "Hungry?"

She was, but clamped her jaw shut anyway and narrowed her eyes out of spite.

"Now, now, don't act like a child."

"Why not? I thought that's what you liked." The words slipped out before she could stop them, and she regretted them when she saw the glint in his watery eyes. It was as though he enjoyed the fact that she knew his dirty little secret and took pleasure in her disgust. They stared at one another for a long moment, then he broke the glare and dipped the spoon into the bowl.

"Open your goddamn mouth." Valentina only looked up at him, one eyebrow partially raised. If he enjoyed her disgust, she too got pleasure from his frustration.

Annoyed, Alan grabbed the back of her head and yanked on her hair. Her head snapped back, hurting her enough to elicit a sharp hiss. "You want to do this the hard way, Miss Tina?"

When he offered her the spoonful again, Valentina accepted it, grimacing at the bitter taste of whatever the hell he just fed her. She didn't know what it was, but certainly didn't want to swallow the grime. So, she did the next best thing.

She spit it directly in his face.

Alan recoiled, fury building in his waxy features. Fear shuddered through Valentina just before he reared back and kicked her injured leg hard, reopening the wound and sending stinging quakes up and down her shin. She couldn't help the short cry of pain that erupted from her. He didn't say another word, just wiped his face and stalked out, leaving Valentina blinking back tears that she refused to let fall.

IT TOOK SOME convincing, but Leo finally got the name of the bar from a deputy at the sheriff's office, the same bar Alan Fredericks was once known to frequent.

Deep down he knew it was a stupid idea, but he was tired of waiting. Leo had no doubt that Barnes and his officers were doing everything in their power to find Valentina, but their power had limitations.

His didn't.

The night after discovering Alan's name, Leo and Dom made their way a few towns over to the bar, a hole in the wall with a dirt parking lot, dimly lit interior, and seedy patrons. Leo was glad he'd brought Dom with him, as his muscle-wrapped friend looked much more fitting than his lanky counterpart. Dom had been eager to tag along and looked forward to feeling out the crowd, getting information out of people one way or the other.

As they entered the bar, Leo let his mind take over, mentally writing the scene. He pictured himself as the lead, a man on the warpath, lusting for vengeance. He wasn't Leo Murdoch, he was the hero saving the damsel in distress – and how would the hero handle this scene?

The pair strode up to the bar and ordered a beer each, then took a seat. They kept to themselves, chatting quietly about nothing important, trying to keep a low profile. Leo glanced around occasionally, frustration building as he realized he had no idea what he was doing, or what clues to search for.

What kind of hero did he want to be? He'd always been the type to sit back and observe, capture the scene perfectly in his mind. But he didn't have the luxury of time or revisions. Valentina needed him now and she needed him to be precise.

Leo gestured to the bartender for another beer. When the bartender, a tall and stocky middle-aged man with long brown hair and a day's worth of scruff, approached, Leo launched into action.

"Thanks," he said as he accepted the beer, then lifted a finger when the man turned to leave. "Can I ask you a question?"

"Shoot." His voice was rough, the single word tinged with a warning neither Leo nor Dom would decipher.

"I'm looking for a man who used to come around here."

The corners of the bartenders turned up in a smirk. "Ain't that kind of bar, man."

Leo refrained from rolling his eyes even as Dom scoffed. "I want to talk to him. His name is Alan. Alan—"

"I know who," the man cut in, his eyes narrowing. "Cops have already been in here asking about him." That surprised Leo, but he kept his mouth shut. "He doesn't come around here anymore. And if you know what's good for you, neither will you."

Leo sat forward. "Look, maybe you don't understand the situation, but—"

"Maybe you don't understand what kind of trouble you're looking for." The bartender kept his voice low, threatening. "You go in a bar and start throwing names around to the wrong person, you might just disappear. I don't know what all this guy is mixed up in, but I can guarantee it's way over your head. Let the cops do the dirty work."

Frustrated, Leo stood, brushing off Dom's hand on his shoulder. "All I need to know is where to find this guy, or where to start looking. I'm not—"

"Bar's closed," the man interrupted, seeming to be careful about not letting others hear him. "Beer's on the house as long as you get the hell out right now."

Leo started to protest, but Dom pulled him away, saying something in his ear about knowing when to back off. The bartender watched them leave, eyes never leaving them until they slipped out the door and made their way back to the car.

"A complete waste of time," Leo muttered as he started the car and pulled out of the parking lot. Dirt flew up behind the tires. "Fucking bartender thinking he's hot shit."

Dom cast his friend a baleful glance. "Leo, that guy probably just saved your life. I know you're new to the whole 'shake down the bad guys at the bar' scene, but think about it. This was a stupid idea anyway."

"Yeah, then why were you so eager to come along?"

"Because I knew you'd need me to drag your ass out before you pissed off the wrong person."

He didn't want to admit it, but Dom was right. Leo

tightened his grip on the steering wheel and clenched his jaw. All he'd accomplished was letting people – perhaps the *wrong* people – know that he was looking for Alan. He could only hope that his actions didn't make things worse for Valentina.

Chapter ELEVEN

THREE DAYS PASSED with no sign of life save for the muffled footsteps above her head. Valentina still sat in the chair, bitter over her capture, starved for food and water, and ashamed by her body's betrayal, no matter her attempts to hold in every possible bodily fluid.

They left her in total darkness, and so she kept herself sane by counting the minutes, though at some point she wondered if she was just making up numbers. At first she kept her eyes open, terrified of what would come for her in the dark, but eventually staring into black air made her sick to her stomach and so instead she hung her head low and closed her eyes, attempting to sleep the nightmare away.

Every part of her ached. Her back and limbs were stiff, her thighs and butt numb, neck sore, wrists and ankles rubbed raw. Her throat was parched and her stomach clenched in a fist of agony. Any movement sent stabbing pain up her spine. She suspected she had a broken rib or two since it hurt to take in air. Any attempt to stretch only made the ropes pull tighter, so finally she tried to stay as still as possible, even when some unknown creature with spindly legs crawled across her exposed leg and knee.

Eventually her head began to nod, but she fought the need to sleep. She was too vulnerable in this position, too helpless, and needed to stay awake to protect herself. But too soon, her mind refused to let coherent thoughts form, though she did manage to curse herself for being so weak.

Perhaps her leg was infected, causing fever. Perhaps she'd lost too much blood, rendering her limbs useless. Perhaps the darkness had finally suffocated her, cutting off her final lifeline.

At some point on the third day, she thought she heard the door open just a crack, feet shuffle against the floor.

Just another hallucination…a dream.

She thought she saw just the dimmest of light and shadow.

There is no light in this place.

She thought she felt hands on her shoulders, moving down across her chest, stomach, legs.

Don't let them win.

She thought she smelled the mustiest of scents coming from somewhere behind her.

You can't let them win.

She thought a lot of things that finally broke her.

UPSTAIRS, HIGH ENOUGH above their captive that their voices wouldn't be heard, the two men argued.

Dane pointed to the small TV that sat on the kitchen counter, the knife in his hand glinting beneath the lights. "You had one job, man! Get the chick and get out! One job!"

"I did my job," Alan answered, the hitch in his voice betraying his otherwise calm tone.

"If you did your job then ya wouldn't have been seen by some idiot jogger!"

"I scouted that route for *weeks*! There was never a jogger, and the neighbors never veered from their schedules. It was a goddamn fluke."

"Yeah, well, that fluke could cost us everything!" Dane tapped the screen with the knife. "They got your picture and name and everything! What the fuck is wrong with you?"

"It's fine!" Alan protested. "What they have is a name and picture of someone who has no ties to this location or house. They will never find us here."

"Still, you gotta take care of that goddamn husband. He's causing more trouble than he's worth."

"Don't you start telling me what to do," Alan seethed. "You are *not* in charge here, and don't you forget that."

"Well then, bossman, looks like you got a job to do." Dane, not at all bothered by the anger in Alan's voice, only waved a hand.

Alan glanced out the window at the baby-faced man walking up the drive. "I have just the person for the job." He waited until the man entered the kitchen, then greeted the new arrival. "We have a job for you."

The man stopped, setting a bag down on the counter, holding back a grimace. "Which store this time?" He couldn't keep the irritation out of his voice. So far he'd been to what felt like every single store in surrounding towns, picking up this or that, making beer runs, keeping his ear to the ground for talk of the kidnappings. He was bored, and tired of being the one the putting his face on the line and risking his identity being discovered, which was why he'd been sure to jump from store to store.

"You ain't getting groceries this time," Dane sneered. "This time you're gonna get your hands dirty."

When the young man sent Alan a questioning look, Alan took over. "The husband. He's been talking to the police. It's time to shut him up."

The man cast a look down to the floor. "That one's husband?" he asked, gesturing to the prisoner below his feet.

"The one and only."

"How do you want me to do it?"

Alan tossed him a gun, sighing when it was fumbled. "You want to earn your stripes, kid? You figure it out. And feed the bitch before you go."

THE LIGHT FLICKED on, sending blinding pain through Valentina's head. She clenched her eyes shut, tears forming that she blinked away. Through blurry vision she watched a figure approach from the side.

A different face stared down at her, one she'd only seen twice before through a thin sack over tired eyes. The nameless young man from her single shower day was before her, an unreadable expression on his face. She didn't say anything, only watched as he squatted down. He was tall, so now he was nearly eye-level with her.

The guy is barely old enough to drink, Valentina managed to think through the fog. *What the hell is he doing here?*

They observed one another, Valentina blinking slowly as she attempted to clear her head, the young man with his brow furrowed almost nervously.

"Uh…my name is John. Guys all call me Johnny. They sent me in here to feed you." His tone was surprisingly soft, his eyes concerned as they looked her up and down. He seemed surprised by how bad she looked, almost sympathetic. "They really worked you over, huh?"

Valentina lifted her head, wishing she had the energy to scoff. Instead she just stared at him balefully until he offered her a small smile and lifted the spoon. She hated the fact that when the food touched her dry lips, she swallowed it and actually wanted more. He fed her slowly, giving her the time she needed to let the food settle. His gentle nature confused her, and as the food and water filled her, Valentina felt her mind working again, plotting to find a way to use his concern against him.

"They shouldn't have hit you," he continued, offering another bite. "The boss won't be happy. Never met him myself, but I hear he's pretty strict about things like that. Not sure why they deviated from the plan." Although he knew he could get in trouble for being so open, it felt good to talk to her, felt good that she was actually listening. "Alan said the boss would give me a lot of money to watch over the house and run a few errands. I needed the money for my mom, to cover her hospital bills. I didn't know it would be for this, though."

Johnny sighed. "It'll be over soon." The promise in his voice was both sad and hopeful. "I heard them say the boss will be here on Monday. You don't have to do this much longer."

She didn't know what day it was, and that frightened her. Monday could be in a week – or it could be tomorrow morning. She would never get out in time if she was strapped to the chair. Something had to be done.

They sat together silently after that, the only sound being the scrape of the spoon against the bowl. When there was no more food or water, Johnny rose to his feet. "Well…I'll be seeing you," he said quietly, offering her a single nod when she just hung her head tiredly. He walked slowly to the door, though she didn't see him cast a glance over his shoulder.

"I was pregnant," Valentina whispered just as his hand touched the door.

"What?"

She didn't lift her head, but did hear him come closer. "I was pregnant." Her voice was rough, throat scratched. "I found out the morning they took me."

Johnny was quiet for a long moment, then came back into view. His forehead was creased with apparent concern.

"Why are you telling me?"

Valentina lifted a tired shoulder, glancing up at the young man, her dirt-smudged face streaked with a single tear. "I never got to tell my husband, or anyone else. I guess... I guess just wanted to tell someone."

He didn't answer, though his expression changed from curious to one of hesitation. When he finally turned on his heel and left, Valentina hid a smile, pleased with the seed of deceit she'd planted in his head.

Chapter TWELVE

DANE CAME FOR her the next day, shoving a burlap bag over her head for no reason other than to piss her off. Despite the previous morning's food, as meager a meal as it was, she was too weak to fight when he untied her and hoisted her to her feet. As soon as he released her, Valentina crashed to the floor, her legs numb.

"Get up," Dane commanded.

I can't, Valentina thought, too tired to speak. She forced her arms beneath her and pushed off the floor, silently ordering her legs to move. Nothing happened, though she did feel the slightest of tingles in her feet.

With a sigh, Dane grabbed hold of her, his massive hand clutching her around the shoulder and underarm. He propped Valentina up and waited until she managed to find some semblance of balance, then shot that balance to hell by dragging her out of the room.

Valentina struggled to make sense of the direction as she was led to the bathroom, committing each step to memory, but after a while she gave up and instead focused on simply keeping her feet under her. Dane wasn't interested in making the walk easy, either.

He all but dumped her in the tub, the thud of her bony body connecting with fiberglass echoing throughout the sparsely-decorated bathroom. Without a word, he turned the shower on. The freezing spray jolted Valentina awake. She climbed to her knees as best she could, collapsing against the lip of the tub for balance while the ice-cold water penetrated her skin, chilling her to the bone. Dane threw soap and shampoo in with her, then stepped back and stood, waiting, at the sink.

Valentina wiped her eyes to clear away the water, fumbling around for the shower knobs. She turned the warm water on, then simply sat for a few minutes, enjoying the feel of thick steam filling her lungs, surrounding her. For a moment, she could almost imagine she was alone in the woods on a muggy day, sunshine hot on her face, taking a dip in summer-warm water.

"Get to it," Dane's voice snapped her out of her daydreaming.

With a heavy sigh, Valentina forced herself to a better sitting position all while wishing she could just lie down and take a nap. The warm water was starting to restore blood flow to the lower half of her body, bringing forth stabbing pains that she gently massaged for a few minutes, trying not to cry.

When Dane barked at her again, she found the soap he'd thrown at her and ran it up and down her arms. Blood, dirt, and filth pooled down the drain from her skin and clothes; she grimaced and turned away from the sight.

Pulling up her pant leg, Valentina tried not to worry when she saw the swollen skin. Her wound wasn't worse, but it certainly wasn't any better. She needed antibiotics, or at least something to help deter whatever infection was starting to spread. Alan had offered her medication at some point but there was no way in hell she was taking a pill from that man.

Soap in hand, Valentina moved to wash her neck and shoulders, reaching beneath the soaked shirt collar. She was surprised by how tender her skin was to the touch, muscles tight and bunched beneath flesh, her neck aching with each pass of the soap.

"You want a massage, you just say the word, sweets."

Valentina scowled over at Dane, who was grinning at her from his place at the sink. Choosing not to reply, she scrubbed her face, careful to avoid the still-healing injuries she'd studied in the mirror the previous day, then moved to her hair. The curly black tresses were so knotted that she couldn't get her fingers through, so she settled for simply letting the shampoo soak in and rinse out.

Too soon, her semi-alone time in the shower ended. Dane growled at her to finish up and she complied, accepting the towel wordlessly and changing into the new clothes as quickly as her limbs would allow. To spite Dane, she left her bra on even though it was wet. She may have been groggy, exhausted, and beaten down, but there was enough spark left in her to defy him in an act of spite. She was forced to forego her soiled underwear, though, which both angered and humiliated her.

Though she felt clean and somewhat rejuvenated, Valentina didn't have the energy to fight when Dane brought her back to the room and retied her to the chair, which someone had cleaned while she was in the shower. Not even when the ropes dug into raw flesh at her wrists did she flinch. It wasn't until he put his hands on her shoulders and squeezed that she tensed, jaw clamping in disgust when he leaned over to whisper in her ear.

"You sit tight til tonight." His breath was hot against her cheek. "The boss'll be here soon, so we're gonna have some fun while Alan is away." He patted her shoulder with a laugh, then straightened and headed for the door.

"And by the way," he said over his shoulder, just before he flicked off the lights, "we sent Johnny boy on an errand. In a few hours, your little lover boy with the big mouth will have shot himself in the head, overcome with grief over your disappearance."

And then he was gone.

Fear filled her senses as she tried to take in Dane's words. Disbelief battled with an overwhelming sense of finality. Any revulsion she may have felt over his promise for the night to come was shoved aside by panic and grief.

Johnny was sent to kill Leo. Johnny, the baby-faced kid she tried to reach with a sob story of a fake pregnancy, was going to murder her husband and make it look like a suicide.

The worst part was, she knew he could do it. These people had skills, whether they looked the part or not. They would take out any and all threats, and that included a man searching for his wife, asking too many questions and getting too close for comfort. Leo wasn't a human being to them. He was just an obstacle to earning their payday – and all obstacles had to be eliminated.

The tears came hard and fast, unstoppable. A sense of loss overcame Valentina, fear for the future, despair for what she couldn't control, hatred for what she'd become. Her weakness, her inability to protect herself, would now lead to Leo's death.

And she couldn't stop it.

She didn't know how long she cried for Leo, how long her sobs echoed around the room, how long she was watched from the corner camera as she struggled against the restraints that cut into her wrists, but eventually, her tears began to dry. Grief faded away to despair, despair faded into acceptance, and with acceptance was born something else entirely. Something cold, something calculating.

Something deadly.

JOHNNY RODE TO the jobsite with the radio blasting, going over the plan in his mind. He knew what he had to do, what Alan had so carefully instructed – what he wasn't sure he could pull off.

Valentina kept clouding his thoughts. The way she looked strapped to the chair, the sadness in her voice when she confessed her secret. How lonely must she have been to share such a thing with one of her captors?

He didn't like seeing a woman like that. He especially didn't approve of the kids being there. If he'd have known it would be like this when he first signed up… Well, maybe he wouldn't have joined at all.

Alan had found him in a bar, drinking his celebratory twenty-first-birthday beer. Johnny was new in town and to that particular bar where Alan had been known to frequent. Looking back on the night, he should have realized how strange it was for Alan to strike up a conversation, asking all sorts of personal questions until he finally got the answer he needed.

"Taking care of my mom," Johnny had replied to his question about why he'd moved to town. "She had a stroke even though she's pretty young, and got put in a shitty nursing home. I want to move her to a better place."

Then came talk of money. Or rather, Johnny mused as his grip tightened on the steering wheel, the words had poured out of him after one too many beers. He'd made it known he was looking for extra work to help pay his mother's medical bills, and thus the offer to "watch the house" had been made.

Johnny took the job thinking he'd be watching the house for a drug dealer, maybe going on a couple runs. That, he could handle. By the time he found out people were being sold, rather than narcotics, it was too late to back out.

Now he was being sent to murder a man who only wanted to find his missing wife. All he knew about Leo Murdoch was that he was getting too close to their trail, and therefore needed to be silenced. Johnny mapped out the kill in his head, already sickened by the thought of blood. He'd never killed anyone, and didn't want to start now.

But if he failed, his mother would pay the price.

Too soon, the drive was over and Johnny was parking the car four streets down from the Murdoch house in a secluded nook in the woods. It was the same spot Alan parked when he watched Valentina, learning her schedule, memorizing her life.

Johnny made the rest of the trip on foot, hands in his pockets, one of which held the gun that would end Leo's life. His eyes never left the dirt path until he came to the woods behind the Murdoch home. It was early still, the sun barely peeking through the trees, the only light coming from the small window in the back of the house that he guessed was the bathroom.

With careful movements perfected after many teenage years of pickpocketing and small-time B&E, Johnny pried open the window leading to the living room, which was dark and empty in the early morning. He entered silently, the quiet unraveling his already fraying nerves, slowly making his way through the tidy house toward the sound of running water.

The bathroom door was ajar, misty steam creeping through the crack. Johnny lifted a gloved hand and pushed it open enough to slip through. Once he entered the small, green-tiled space, he could see a slight shadow on the other side of the shower curtain. His hand trembled as he lifted the gun; he forced his nerves to stay calm, bracing his wrist with his other hand until the shaking stopped. Taking in a deep breath, Johnny reached out and shoved the curtain back.

The scream from the woman in the shower startled him enough that he stumbled back, hitting the countertop hard.

"Who–who the fuck are you?" he stammered, staring at the naked middle-aged woman before him.

"Who the fuck are *you*?" she shouted back. Her eyes widened when they landed on the gun. "*Leo!*"

Johnny raised a hand when she leapt out of the shower and started pummeling him with her fists, not bothering to cover herself. She clawed and slapped, kneed him hard when he attempted to get away.

"Who are you?" she yelled again, then gasped when he regained his composure and pointed the gun dead center at her face.

"Get back!" Johnny demanded, desperately trying to think of how he was going to get out of this situation. "I don't want to kill you!"

And he didn't. He didn't even want to kill Leo, but that was the job. This woman, whoever the hell she was, wasn't part of the plan, and hell if he was going to have *two* innocent lives on his conscience.

"You, just...stay there," he ordered with a shaky voice. He turned to dart out of the bathroom and was knocked back by the fist that plowed directly into his chin.

A pair of strong hands grabbed for the gun, but Johnny had grown up fighting and wasn't one to end up on his back after a single punch. He landed two quick hits to his opponent's gut and cheek, hard enough to free himself and get some distance. Gun raised, he backed out of the bathroom.

"Don't even try it," he warned Leo, who had taken a step forward.

"Who are you? Did *they* send you?" he asked.

"Don't you worry about who sent me."

"Do you know where Valentina is?"

The tough-guy façade fell away at that, and Johnny saw the distinct change in Leo's expression when he realized who the stranger holding the gun may be. Despite himself, Johnny felt a pang of pity for the man. "You've been making a lot of trouble for people, man."

Leo heard the hitch in his voice. He struggled to stay calm, to try to reason with the young man holding the gun. "Look, no one has to know you were here. Just tell me where to find my wife. That's all I care about."

Johnny shook his head, adjusting his grip on the gun as he shuffled from foot to foot. "You don't get it, man. She ain't coming back."

"What do you mean?" Leo asked, panic in his voice. "Is she still alive?

Johnny ignored the question, glancing at the woman behind Leo when she whimpered, then back at Leo. "You shoulda kept your mouth shut."

Leo held up his hands in a peace offering. "We never saw you, man. Never. You tell us where to find Valentina, that she's alive, and you can just disappear."

Johnny scoffed. "Man, I'm gonna disappear no matter what happens to you or your wife." But something held him back. Perhaps it was the look of pure terror in the woman's eyes. Maybe it was the panic mixed with sheer determination in Leo's. Whatever it was, Johnny knew these people weren't a threat.

He started to speak, but then Leo moved.

Panic had Johnny pulling the trigger.

The woman screamed Leo's name, but Johnny didn't stick around to see if the bullet found its mark. He turned on his heel and raced back through the house, leaping out the window and darting through the woods until he made it to the safety of his car. Once there, he went the opposite direction of the house where Valentina was still imprisoned.

Whether or not he'd succeeded in killing Leo Murdoch, Johnny had been serious when he said he was going to disappear. His mother was ready to go home, and the first payment Alan had given him the day before was going to make sure they found a new home as far away from the west coast as they could get.

Back inside the house, Lillian dropped to the floor next to Leo, clutching a towel around her body. "Leo? Answer me!"

Leo sat up, surprised to find himself alive. It took him a moment to register the fact that he was sitting on the bathroom floor. Pain pounded in his hip, and he looked down to see a shallow laceration just above the waistline of his boxers.

"Shit," he whispered, gazing down at his blood-coated fingers. "I think it just grazed me." A quick look behind him showed the bullet lodged into the wall.

"You were lucky."

Leo turned his gaze to Lillian, whose eyes were filled with tears. "*We* were lucky." The kid clearly had no way of knowing Lillian would be in the shower, or even in the house, which meant he'd been looking for Leo. They were both fortunate that the young man had obviously been nothing more than a lackey, and one who wanted out of the operation at that.

Lillian helped Leo to his feet. "What do we do now?"

He took the washcloth she handed him and held it to his side. "Well…we know Val is alive. He said he would disappear no matter what happens to me or my wife, not what *happened*. That's got to mean she's still alive." He sighed and set the red-tinted cloth down. "We just don't know for how much longer."

Chapter
THIRTEEN

IN THE DARK, Valentina waited.

She felt empty inside, unable to care about the gloomy thoughts crossing her mind and tainting her soul. Images of death and destruction, war and murder, filled her vision. Everything she'd lost – her freedom, her future, MoMo, Leo – consumed what was left of her spirit, letting a frightening kind of hopelessness settle into her bones. She wanted to survive, but only so she could destroy.

Nothing matters after that.

In her depression, she barely noticed that the light wasn't on, didn't give The Midnight Man even a moment's thought. He couldn't haunt a fractured mind – and Valentina was sure that her mind was very, very broken.

Instead of letting her childhood nightmare creep its way back into her life, she pictured what she would do, what she *must* do, when the time came.

She bided that time carefully, listening to the sounds above. She identified male voices in the room over her head, and it annoyed her that more people had entered the mix when she'd planned on only two. At some point, she heard the scratch of tires against rock that signified Alan leaving…likely to bring back someone else since the boss was due to arrive soon. Part of her hoped he was bringing another person to the house rather than taking one of the children away to their untimely death.

As promised, not long after Alan left, Dane appeared.

Her head cocked to the side ever so slightly when the lock scraped against the door. Her breath was even, nerves calm, heartbeat strangely under control.

He turned on the light, stepping inside and closing the door behind him. She didn't turn, though those calm nerves began to curdle in her gut, clenching into fists of fire when she heard the lock latch from the outside.

That's not part of the plan.

She hadn't considered he would get someone to lock the door behind him. Then again, she hadn't planned on the other men being there either. Accommodations needed to be made to her plan, and fast.

"Just me and you, sweets," Dane said, a laugh tinting his voice. "They'll come get us out when I'm good and ready."

Valentina swallowed hard, hands bunching. She fought to keep herself still when he ran his fingers down her arms, stopping at her wrists. He untied her, only to re-bind her hands in front of her.

"You'll need those," he explained with malice in his grin. Then he freed her legs and easily lifted her to her feet, her listless body following orders. Her head spun when he twirled her around, crushing her fragile body to his. He reeked of cigarettes and beer and…excitement, she thought with an inward sigh.

The thought must have reflected on her face, because Dane lifted a hand and used it to grab her by the chin. He jerked her head until she was forced to look at him.

"You try anything, sweetheart, and I promise you'll live long enough to regret it."

He led her to the mattress, a grin crossing his weather- and drug-worn face when he untied her pants. They fell to the floor, forgotten, and still she didn't move. Her dull and vacant eyes stared at the ground, face emotionless.

Dane shoved her onto her back by the shoulders, then stood over her. "Been waiting for this, haven't ya?" He lowered himself to his knees, pulling his favored knife out of his back pocket. "I sure as shit know I have. And you ain't gonna say a word to the boss, are ya?" The edge of his knife traced along her cheekbone. "'Cuz ya know what'll happen if you been tainted before he gets his hands on ya."

Bile rose in the back of her throat as he pushed her bound arms up over her head. Her eyes watered when he moved his hand to her throat, squeezing hard enough to send a silent threat. So she didn't move, not when he worked a hand up her shirt, not when he kissed her bare hip. Her legs were jelly when he pushed them aside, moving his head between her knees.

And when he positioned himself just right, she moved.

With a speed that surprised even her, Valentina clamped her legs together, catching Dane by the head and neck. With every ounce of strength she had, she twisted and thrashed, slamming her arms down onto the back of his head, realizing too late that breaking someone's neck wasn't as easy as it looked in the movies. Her teeth smashed together as she struggled to tighten her hold, her thighs quivering as her mind cursed Hollywood for making it look so simple.

Dane shouted in rage and pain, dropping the knife and grabbing at her legs. His fingers dug into her flesh, pulling himself free, jerking back just enough that Valentina was able to land a hard kick to his nose, then another to his groin, one right after the other with her bare heels connecting solidly. He doubled over, bracing himself against the floor with one hand, giving her enough time to scramble off the mattress and grab the abandoned knife.

She eyed Dane now, holding out the knife cautiously as

he pulled himself up, knowing she looked like a ridiculous amateur. Despite her trembling hands, which were still bound together tightly, she pictured herself finishing him off, shoving her hand forward and letting the blade bite through skin.

When Dane stumbled forward, she had the chance to do just that, but something held her back. Valentina cursed herself for stepping back and hesitating long enough to give him a chance to catch his balance. The simple truth was, no matter what she envisioned herself doing, no matter how long and hard she thought about doing it, she wasn't a killer. She'd never done anything even close to stabbing a person.

"You ain't gonna do it," Dane rasped, blood dripping from his nose. Everything he wanted to do to her, the pain he was desperate to cause, was written clearly across his face. "You just signed your death warrant, bitch."

"Then I've got nothing to lose," she answered, her tone just as deadly. The resignation in her voice registered with Dane, who wiped at his nose and flung a string of blood at her feet. They both sneered at the move.

"You want me," Valentina challenged, "come and get me."

When he rushed forward, she didn't allow herself to think.

The knife pressed into Dane's gut smoothly, too smoothly, she managed to think. It pushed in to the handle; only the sound of Dane's yelp indicated that the blood flowing over her hand wasn't her own.

He fought against her, pure adrenaline fueling his limbs. One blow landed to her forehead, another to her jaw, and what felt like an elbow struck her in the mouth. Still Valentina held her stance, pushing her fist against his stomach, twisting a little more with each hit her body endured. She buried her head in Dane's shoulder to avoid his fists, breath whooshing from her when he crushed her body to his with a surprisingly strong arm.

But then the fight left him and he sank to his knees with a grunt.

Could it be that easy? she asked herself, watching the man fall to his side while holding his stomach. The figure that once looked so intimidating and hulking was now a quivering mess at her feet – and the sight satisfied her.

In fact, it more than satisfied her. It made her downright happy.

Valentina stood still as a statue until Dane stopped moaning and jerking. Her eyes never left him, taking in the sight of his gaping mouth with blood dribbling from the corners, his hands that clenched and unclenched, his right foot that twitched oddly. Until finally, all movements ceased. There was no question that he was dead, for the pool of blood surrounding him was a clear testament to his lack of life.

Her question was barely discernible when she whispered, "What the hell do I do now?"

Run, Forrest. Get out.

She hurried to the mattress and picked up her pants, pulling them on at record speed. With a huff she realized her wrists were still bound, and she wasted precious minutes using the bloody knife to cut through the ropes before running to the door, smearing blood around the frame as she tugged at the handle. It was locked, not budging even an inch, and only then did she remember what Dane said – they'd get him out when he was good and ready. The bastard had locked it from the outside and now she was trapped inside with a dead man.

Fuck.

She knew she had to act fast. Someone would see what she'd done and come for her – which was ultimately what she wanted, albeit when she was more prepared. Despite her exhaustion, she was filled with a sense of urgency and excitement. She'd killed one, and would destroy the others out of pure spite for what had been done to her, to Leo, to the kids.

But they would see her, know what she was doing. They would come in with their weapons drawn and gun her down where she stood. She had to get the upper hand.

Hand.

Valentina glanced down at the blood covering her palm, then slowly turned her gaze to the mirror. Only then did she wonder if anyone had been watching all along, or if, by some stroke of luck, the others in the house had been away from the camera.

An idea struck, disgusting as it was, and she didn't hesitate to drag the chair over to the corner. It was heavier than she'd expected – or perhaps she was now that weak – and by the time she had the chair settled she was almost out of breath.

She stepped on the seat and hoisted herself up, now nearly eye level with the center of the mirror. Lifting a hand, she dragged it across the surface, smearing red.

The blood wasn't thick enough. With a grimace, Valentina jumped down and walked back to Dane's lifeless form. She swallowed back sickness as she reached down and pressed her hands into warm blood, refusing to look even as she wiped them across the mirror. The bitter metallic smell accosted her senses, but she made trip after trip, dripping red all over the floor and herself, until the mirror was coated with a thick red glaze.

Satisfied with her work, Valentina cast a final glance at the mirror then marched back to Dane's body and searched his pockets. All she found was a tattered wallet with ten dollars and a faded license, a pack of cigarettes, and a lighter. Suddenly exhausted after ransacking his clothing, she tossed the wallet aside and settled down against the wall, just beneath the mirror, with Dane's knife in hand.

Chapter
FOURTEEN

And waited.

SHE THOUGHT THEY'D come quickly, rushing to save their friend who lay motionless on the cold concrete floor, but she waited so long that boredom was setting in. Valentina hadn't moved from her spot along the wall, her eyes trained on the body, her left hand gripping the knife. While she waited, she thought about what to do next, how to escape a throng of men who would happily kill her.

Unless she killed them first.

But could she? Dane was dead because he was actively trying to hurt her. Stabbing him had been as much an accident as it had been on purpose, and he'd partly walked into the blade thinking she wouldn't have the guts to hold it between them. Could she do the same to someone who was just walking down the stairs, sitting at the kitchen table, standing in the hallway?

They turned you into this.

That made her blood boil more than anything else. Alan, Dane, the boss – they made her a killer, forced her to spill blood in order to protect herself. They had no one to blame but themselves for what would happen to them, for what had already happened to Dane.

His blood had dried on her hands. The skin around her fingers was stiff, bits of red flaking off when she unclenched her fists. It felt good to have someone else's blood on her, to know she was more powerful than the enemy.

Valentina was ripped from her thoughts by the sound of voices shouting. They were urgent – and getting louder. They were coming for her.

Heavy footsteps pounded on the stairs, but oddly, she realized after listening carefully, only one set. She rose to her feet slowly, pressing her ear against the wood paneling when the footsteps slowed and eventually came to a stop on the other side of the room.

"Dane?" a muffled male voice called through the door. The person knocked lightly. "What the fuck you do to the camera? We said we wouldn't watch."

Valentina stood stone still, barely even breathing.

"Yo, Dane! You okay, man?" The man knocked again, the sound causing Valentina's nerves to stand on end. Her right hand started to shake, so she pressed it against the wall for support.

"Dane! What the fuck, man, I'm coming in."

Valentina sucked in a breath as the man on the other side of the door began working the lock. The door opened inward, her standing just behind the solid wood. Her eyes were trained on the floor, and when she saw the figure's foot appear, she sprang into action.

Valentina rounded the door with lightning speed, arcing her fist around and up, eyes closed at what she was about to do.

The figure saw her coming a second too late, throwing up his arms in defense just as the knife buried itself in his stomach. He didn't cry out or fight, instead stumbling forward while casting an incredulous look her way. Valentina yanked the knife from his body and watched him fall, barely comprehending what she'd done. Survival mode had kicked in, not allowing her to feel regret or shame or disgust, only a strange kind of grim satisfaction.

The man slid to his hands and knees, blood dripping to the floor from his wound and the corners of his mouth. Valentina helped him down the rest of the way, kicking him in the back so that he tumbled to his side next to Dane's lifeless form. He reached out for her feebly, fingers grazing her bare ankle as she darted around the door, closing it softly.

Now on the outside, she saw how they were keeping her locked in. The door was a work of art, made of thick wood on either side, a sturdy metal frame, and an intricate lever contraption that she simply stared at for a moment. Then she slammed the lever down so that it crossed the entire door and secured it shut with the padlock on the end. Even if the man ended up surviving, he wouldn't get out.

Suddenly free of her cage, Valentina found herself at a loss, unsure how to continue. She was barefoot, clothes stained red, hair a mess, stomach growling. A half-starved, half-delirious woman wouldn't get far in a house of bad guys – and she was literally bringing a knife to a gunfight.

Valentina glanced around the dim basement, annoyed by how little was actually there. The space was expansive, stretching far from wall to wall, and yet, there was hardly anything to see. There were two narrow windows against the far wall, boarded up from the outside. The rest of the walls were bare, albeit water stained with mold inching its way across the baseboards. What looked like a water heater was in the corner, though Valentina wasn't sure how it managed to work judging by the amount of rust coating the metal.

A few feet away from the heater sat a pile of boxes. She searched them quickly, finding only old clothes. Her stomach churned at the thought of those clothes possibly belonging to past victims, and she wondered if the rags she wore now had once been stripped off another woman.

Next to the box of clothes was what looked like a car part. Valentina attempted to pick up the rusted metal, but found it heavier than she expected.

Find a weapon you can actually carry.

With a sigh, Valentina abandoned the car part and continued her search around the basement, all while keeping a close watch on the stairs. Aside from the boxes now at her back, the floor was bare.

Then her eyes landed on a pipe as long as her forearm to fingertips.

That'll do, she thought tiredly, retrieving the pipe, inwardly cursing herself at the sound of metal dragging against concrete. The noise seemed to echo all around the basement. Pausing long enough to ensure she was still alone, Valentina started to creep up the stairs, one slow step at a time, her eyes trained on the door.

When she reached the top, Valentina stopped. She slipped the knife into her pocket, deciding that for the immediate future, the pipe was the better weapon of choice since it offered a longer reach. For a moment she stood with her ear pressed against the door, but she didn't hear anything, not even muffled voices from the people she knew were still in the house.

Almost silently, willing her hands to stay steady, Valentina eased the door open, relieved it was unlocked. She slipped out and closed the door behind her quietly, then looked up and down the hall. Only once had they let her see this hallway, albeit through a thin sack over her head, and she remembered being taken down the right to the bathroom. But she also recalled coming in from the left on that first awful day.

Valentina turned and slowly padded down the hall, keeping a sharp ear out for any sounds. From somewhere deep in the huge house she heard a man laugh; she stopped long enough to assure that laugh wasn't headed her way. Even after the house went silent again, she still pressed herself against the wood paneling, afraid that any move she made would echo down the hall.

Her aching stomach eventually drove her forward, the need for food and freedom getting her moving. She had to get out of here. She had to escape the hell of the past... She didn't even know how many days had passed since her kidnapping.

Her memory served her well, masked as it was at the time of her kidnapping by fear, pain, and despair. She crept through the house, keeping to the wall, breaths shallow and almost silent. The tight grip on the pipe never faltered, even when she peered around hallways, seeing only empty rooms that she didn't care to explore.

It didn't seem real that she was actually making her way through the house, step by careful step. After so long in that room, tied to the chair, shivering in the dark, she felt like someone else still had control of her limbs. Perhaps her inner hero was guiding her, showing her where to turn, helping her along the way. Tunnel vision had taken over, though her ears were open to any and every sound around her.

In her mind she counted the footsteps until finally, with bated breath, she turned another corner and saw her freedom only two paces away – the front door.

Elation flooded Valentina, revitalizing every exhausted part of her. Not able to stop the grin that stretched across her tired and pale face, she rushed forward, bare feet hardly making a sound on the wood floors. Free. She was free. The door was right there, waiting to be opened. No one was there to stop her. No one was *going* to stop her.

Valentina reached for the doorknob, fingertips touching metal, mind already planning her race to the woods to hide in the shadows of night. But then, another thought made her freeze in place.

There are children here.

She could still get out. She could still escape. Run through the woods, find people. Find help. There was no one around to make her stay.

There are children here.

The police would come back for the kids. She would lead them back here, cops with their guns drawn, furious villagers with pitchforks if need be.

There are children here.

She'd been put through hell. Tortured, abused, starved, stabbed. She deserved freedom. She deserved to be at peace with whatever life awaited her outside these walls.

There are children here.

It wasn't her job to save anyone. She wasn't a hero. She never asked for this. She never wanted to take care of anyone but herself.

There are children *here.*

Valentina's eyes closed briefly, her hand tightening on the doorknob, twisting it ever so slightly as her thoughts wrestled with one another. Her body ached from the guttural internal scream she let loose in her mind. She was close, so close, to escaping. All she had to do was open the door, step outside, and run.

Run.

Her hand left the doorknob, fingers dropping off the metal regretfully. A sigh of resignation bubbled up in her chest. There was no escape for cowards, only for those worthy of freedom. A woman who left behind innocent lives to suffer the consequences of her actions was no woman of worth.

I'm sorry, Mom.

Eyes opening, back straightening, Valentina turned and walked deeper into the house.

Chapter FIFTEEN

AT THE SHERIFF'S insistence, Leo got his wound cleaned and stitched up at the hospital. His anxiety grew the longer he was there until finally they cleared him to go home. First, he and Lillian stopped at the police station.

"He was in my goddamn house, Barnes," Leo opened, slamming a fist down on the desk. "They're watching us. I don't know how, but they are. And they want to shut us up."

"Not us," Sheriff Barnes replied. "You." When Leo deflated just a bit, the older man sighed. "You said yourself the kid hesitated when he realized it was Lillian was in the shower. He wasn't there for her. He was there for you, only you. And why? Because you did exactly what I told you *not* to do, and went out looking for the bad guys."

Barnes lifted a hand when Leo sucked in a breath, getting ready to respond. "I'm not finished. So what happened next? The bad guys found you instead. And now you're barging in here demanding answers for questions *you* started asking. Sound about right?" He waited for a response, but Leo only stood on the other side of the desk, arms crossed in defiance though his eyes held the slightest hint of shame behind his glasses.

"Listen, Leo. We are doing what we can. It's bad enough that Valentina was taken. We can't have you putting yourself at risk, or Lillian. You need to let us do our jobs, and you running around putting your nose where it doesn't belong is going to get your wife killed." Barnes saw the fear register.

Leo swallowed hard, ignoring Lillian when she attempted to take his hand in a gesture of comfort. "So, what happens next?"

"Next," Barnes gestured to two officers who stood just outside his office, "you two go home, and you stay there."

Leo glanced over his shoulder. "Who… Wait. Are you putting us under house arrest? You don't have the right to do that."

"I can't make you stay, but I can damn sure make sure that no matter what you do, you're being watched and followed. Try sneaking around bars and getting information with three cops standing over your shoulder." Barnes crossed his arms as well when the officer was joined by two more. "Go home. Get some rest. We've got your testimony and a sketch of the kid. We've got fingerprints, though my guess is the kid doesn't have a record and that's why he's the one doing the dirty work. Let me do my job and find Valentina, without having to worry about you too."

Leo started to protest, but was cut off by Lillian's insistent urge. "No, Leo, he's right. We've done enough. It's in their hands now."

It took him a few minutes, but Leo finally managed to drag himself out of the station, head hung low. Although deep down he knew the sheriff was right, he couldn't help but feel that, yet again, he'd failed his wife.

SHE DIDN'T GO back the way she came. Instead, Valentina toured the house, not impressed by the sparse furnishing. In fact, most rooms were nearly bare. This obviously wasn't a house used for actual living, and she guessed the only rooms that held furnishings were the kitchen and living room – and those holding captives.

A musty smell emitted from the walls, telling of the house's age. Paint was peeling from the doorframes, bits of ceiling caved in around the corners, the floor buckled from what she guessed was water damage. The old wood paneling was faded and cracked, bowed out in some places. Briefly she wondered who owned the house and if they knew the place was being used for human trafficking, and hoped that by the end of this, she could have the place bulldozed just for what it stood for. What was once a beautiful house was now a mold-infested hellhole that needed a fresh start.

Valentina stopped when she reached the kitchen. It was a small space with brown-tiled floors and yellow cabinets that may have once been white. The refrigerator was lined with rust, but appeared to be in working order, though she doubted the stove did much more than hold the empty beer bottles currently cluttering the top.

When she stepped in the room, she realized the men's voices were closer now; she guessed they were in the next room. The thought terrified her, but that terror was soon replaced by eagerness when she saw a bag of bread on the counter.

Valentina rushed to the counter, holding the pipe between her knees as she carefully worked to open the bag. Panic rose when the bag crinkled but still she pressed on, driven by the need for sustenance. She could already taste the bread, feel the grains between her teeth. The illusion was so enticing that her mouth started to water.

Footsteps halted her attempts. Begrudgingly, Valentina abandoned the bread and ducked down against the side of the counter. The rapid movement sent spikes of pain up her injured leg, but she pressed her lips together and ordered herself to stay quiet.

Heavy boots thudded into the kitchen, stopping at the fridge. She risked a glance around the corner, eyes widening at the tall and wide-framed man who was bending over to grab a cold beer. His hair was close-cropped, neck merged with broad shoulders, pants hanging halfway off his backside. She didn't see a weapon. There were only seconds to decide what to do, and because not thinking had served her well so far, Valentina simply reacted.

She rose from her hiding place silently, straightening slowly as though uncurling from a long rest, bare feet not making a sound over the beer bottles clanging together in the fridge. Just as the man straightened, Valentina swung the pipe as hard as she possibly could, connecting with the back of his shaved head.

To her surprise, the man fell backwards, right on top of her. The pipe almost slipped from her hands as she struggled to catch both him and herself, failing miserably. They tumbled to the floor, the man's dead weight crushing her brittle body. Valentina bit back a cry when her elbow connected with the hard floor, jarring her shoulder. Though, she wouldn't have been able to cry out anyway due to the pressure bearing down on her chest.

The beer bottle fell from the man's grasp as they fell, shattering against the tile. Valentina grimaced, glancing around for any new figures that may come to investigate.

"What are you doing in there?" a voice called out from the other room, tinted with humor. "You break it, you buy it!"

Valentina struggled to breathe beneath the weight, swallowing back dry heaves at the warm blood dripping onto her neck from the man's head wound. She knew he wasn't dead by the quiet moans he emitted, and that worried her. Soon he would wake up enough to cry for help, and she'd be a sitting duck – or a crushed one, she managed to think with a roll of her eyes.

Shimmy and slide, or wait for them to kill you.

Inch by inch she eased out from beneath the man, out of breath by the time she had her upper half free. The knife wound in her leg screamed with every movement and she felt it tear open, a sob of pain escaping before she could clamp her free hand over her mouth.

"Tubs?" the same voice called out again. "What the fuck is going on, man?"

"Shit," Valentina muttered, yanking her injured leg free with one final gasp. She cast a quick glance down at the half-unconscious man. For good measure, she lifted the pipe high above her head, intending to hit him again. Hesitation had her flexing her fingers on the metal before she slammed the pipe down on his forehead – just in case he decided to wake up.

"Hey!"

Her head jerked up and she looked through sweaty strands of hair at the man standing in the doorway, beer in one hand and gun in the other. Instinct had her leaping for the other doorway, her back hitting the opposing wall just as a bullet slammed into the counter where she'd been leaning. The man shouted for someone else – briefly she prayed there were only two more – but she didn't wait around to see who was coming for her. She was already surprised by how many people had showed up at the house, and didn't want to think of what that may mean.

Valentina pushed herself off the wall and crawl-limped into a room just off the hallway, slamming the door shut with her foot. The pipe fell to the floor with a clang, but she didn't retrieve it. Instead she searched for a hiding place, but like the others, this room was bare, giving her only the door to hide behind.

"Call Alan!" one of the men shouted. "Tell him the bitch got loose!"

Shit, Valentina thought frantically, wincing as she got to her knees. Alan coming back meant one more adversary to get past, and she had a feeling he wouldn't be his typically calm self when he saw what she had done to the others.

"Get the bitch!" the other one yelled, his voice farther away. A lucky break, Valentina managed to think just as the door opened slowly. Quickly, she pulled the knife from her pocket, and when she saw a sneakered foot cross the threshold, she slammed the blade down.

A guttural howl erupted from the man as he stumbled back. Valentina shoved the door into him, sending him tumbling into the hallway. The gun dropped from his hand and slid across the floor. Knowing it was likely a foolish move, she rounded the door and raced for the gun, both of them grappling for the weapon. Fists and elbows flew, connecting with flesh in bruising blows. Two sets of hands were on the gun, Valentina struggling with her back to the man's chest, the man snarling and working an arm around her throat.

Air whooshed from her lungs when that arm tightened. Valentina momentarily forgot the gun and instead focused on breathing and getting free from his grasp. Her windpipe closed, crushed under the weight of his arm. She kicked out, trying to get leverage over him, but found only slippery floor beneath her feet.

"You…are gonna…pay," the man grunted out, holding her against him with one arm and grabbing for the gun with the other. Blood seeped from his foot, which was all but useless now. "Just wait…til Alan gets a hold of you."

The thought of Alan doing just that had Valentina panicking. Her fingers clawed at his arm as she gasped for air, lungs burning. A veil began to cloud her thoughts. Her legs were worthless in this fight and her hands were busy trying to pry the arm from around her throat.

You have a mouth, don't you?

The idea struck and Valentina sank her teeth into the man's forearm, biting down as hard as she could until she tasted blood. The man howled and released her enough for her to scramble away, sucking in a much-needed breath of air. A fast glance at his arm showed a satisfactory gash where she'd ripped through skin.

The fight commenced without either saying a word, both man and woman leaping for the gun. Stars spotted Valentina's vision and she relied on her other senses to help her, shoving herself against the man when he picked up the weapon and started to point it in her direction. Finally, with a snarl of frustrated effort, she got her arm twisted around his.

Locked together in battle, both at an equal disadvantage with injured legs, the two began their final struggle. They fell into the hall, each trying to out-strength the other. The man clearly had the advantage there, but Valentina was crafty, maneuvering herself in a way that had her body twisted around his so that he couldn't tear away from her. Shoving her arm between his elbow and side, she finally felt the hard metal gun in her hands, but couldn't tell which direction the barrel was facing. Nor could she determine whose finger was on the trigger, who had the upper hand.

She didn't have time to wonder, because without warning, the gun went off.

Valentina stumbled back, falling flat on her ass, the man doing the same. She hit the floor hard and slumped to her elbows before managing to pick herself up. Frantically, she searched her body, hands prying for a wound. She was in so much pain already that she didn't think she'd be able to tell a gunshot from any other injury.

A groan from her enemy broke her search, and she looked up to see him collapsed against the ground, hand pressed to the side of his neck as he tried to stop the rush of blood. But it was too late, and they both knew it. Valentina could only watch as the man tried desperately to save himself, the look in his eyes almost pleading, and for a moment she felt the slightest bit of pity while wondering if it had been her finger that pulled the trigger, or if it all truly was an accident.

It doesn't matter. He's the enemy.

She knew she shouldn't care, but it wasn't easy seeing someone die right before her eyes, to actually be able to see the light and life leave his eyes.

Soon the man was just a body twitching on the floor. Valentina stared at him incredulously, hands glued to the gun. He marked the third man she'd taken down. Part of her knew it wasn't supposed to be this easy. She wasn't a fighter and barely knew how to punch. Either she'd been supremely lucky, these guys just weren't trained to kill, or fate was gearing her up for one hell of a final battle.

Her head snapped to one of the only windows not covered when she heard a car starting. She limped into the kitchen and over to the window, peering through the midnight darkness to see another man, who she guessed to be the one calling Alan, speeding away down the driveway. Headlights flashed over the driveway as tires skidded over gravel.

Coward, she thought wryly, pleased yet also wary. If he was running, it wasn't because he was afraid of her.

She had to get out before the real terror arrived.

Picking herself up off the counter, Valentina used the wall as a brace and hurried – as well as she could – to the next room. She found herself in the living room, which she had passed only twice before going to the bathroom. Glancing in, she saw the ugly faded couch as well as a table with monitors. Curiosity got the better of her and she entered, all but falling into the seat.

"Son of a bitch," Valentina muttered, looking over all

five monitors. One showed the front porch, which currently was empty and lit only by a dim overhead light. A second was trained on the back porch. She knew they were night-vision cameras by the greenish tint, allowing her to see into the pitch black of night.

The monitor in the center looked blurry, and it took her a moment to realize that was her room and the blur was, in fact, Dane's own blood that she had smeared across the glass. Her suspicions had been correct. They could see every inch of her room, and through the smeared blood she could just make out two dark forms, one right next to the other. Dane and the other man hadn't moved.

Serves you right, she thought smugly.

Then her eyes moved to the remaining two monitors sitting side-by-side, and her heart sunk.

The screen on the right looked into a small, cramped room. She guessed the light was off based on the green tint, but still could see a small lump on the bed that she guessed was a child huddled beneath a thin blanket. A toilet was in the far corner, the only other item in the room.

The screen on the left was a little dimmer. Valentina squinted, able to see a bed, but it was empty. She searched the grainy screen and finally saw a shadow huddled in the corner, wrapped in what she guessed was a blanket.

Two children. Ally and Samuel, if the news was right. Other children had been taken before them, she remembered hearing, but if these monitors had any say in the matter, Valentina feared it was too late for them. Whatever these children were kidnapped for, the others had already suffered the impending fate.

She could save these two.

Rising from the chair, exhausted, hungry, and flat-out furious, Valentina began her search through the house.

Chapter
SIXTEEN

"YOU GOTTA GET back to the house *now*!"

Alan pulled the phone away from his ear at the frantic shout. "Calm down, for fuck's sake. What's wrong?" He sat back in the booth of the seedy bar, far in the corner away from prying eyes. From that spot he could keep a careful eye on everyone coming and going, though for the most part the faces were the same. It was the same bar where he'd picked up Johnny and brought him into the operation.

He liked to think of the bar as his place, his favorite place, especially considering the strip joint next door that had no problem hiring underage girls in need of extra cash. It was out of the way, off the main road, and even served up decent appetizers.

Right now, though, his good mood was quickly being soured.

"The chick got out. She somehow got past Dane and knocked the shit outta Tubs. I think they're dead, man!"

Alan sat up straighter, hand tightening around his beer. "Where is she?"

"She got out! We found her in the kitchen. She coulda walked right out the door and we never would have known but the crazy bitch came back for more. She's lost it, man."

Alan knew better. The woman wasn't insane. She was annoyingly tough, hard to break. She could have run, but she knew the truth – they had kids locked up in the house. He rose and tossed a few bills on the table. "I'm on my way." Then he paused, listening to the background noise. "Where the hell are you?"

"That bitch is insane," the man replied. "She took out Tubs with a damn pipe and went full-on wrestling with Jim for the gun. I didn't sign up to get shot to pieces by a nut-job. She's all yours."

Rage stiffened his back, though he wasn't surprised by the cowardice. The men they hired were only temporary, and for the most part, they seemed to catch on that when the job was done, so too were they. This one wouldn't be the first who tried to run.

"I'll deal with the bitch. The boss will deal with you."

SHE MADE HER way through the large house slowly, all but dragging her leg behind her. Each hallway seemed to stretch with every step, taunting her pain. Not knowing where the kids were, too afraid to call out lest she catch the attention of an enemy in hiding, Valentina could only take the house one room at a time. It was only now that she realized just how big the house was; with each empty room the minutes ticked by.

Alan would be coming for her.

The boss would be coming for her.

She had to hurry.

Every time she saw a light switch, she flicked it on. It may have been foolish to turn on every light in the house, even the rooms she didn't enter, but it was a force of habit. Valentina hated the dark, and the longer it took her to find the kids, the more the dim lights started to fray her nerves. Even though she was equipped with a knife, pipe, and gun – two of which were in her baggy pockets – she still felt powerless and exposed in the shadows.

Soon, she came to a staircase bathed in darkness. Valentina took in a deep breath, staring up the steps with trepidation. She thanked whatever angels were watching over her that there was another light switch on the wall that lit the way to the third floor.

It was difficult moving up, having to boost each step by leaning on the railing. She had to take her time, as precious as time was, and the sweat beading along her brow was testament to just how many difficulties that staircase gave her.

At the top of the stairs, Valentina came to two closed doors.

Gotcha.

Something told her she would find the children behind those doors. She had no way of knowing which child was behind which door, so she went for the closest room since it didn't matter anyway – she was going to get them both.

The door wasn't as heavily locked as hers, perhaps because the men didn't worry about children being able to escape as easily as a grown woman. There was just a padlocked doorknob without a key, and the pipe in Valentina's hand to break it off.

She lifted the pipe and slammed it down hard on the doorknob, no longer caring if she was heard. Again and again the pipe struck metal until finally the knob snapped off. It took some finagling, but Valentina finally jarred the door open and stepped inside, snapping on the light switch on the outside wall.

The smell reached her first, an odor of filth mixed with mold and must. Then her eyes adjusted and took in the rustling on the bed. The small form tried to shrink into itself, a tiny whimper coming from under the blanket. The sound nearly brought tears to Valentina's eyes as she approached cautiously, not wanting to frighten the child.

"Hello?" she asked, feeling stupid. She didn't know

how to talk to kids, especially ones who were being held captive and likely suspected her of being another bad guy. "My... My name is...Tina," she went for the easiest name. "I'm here to help."

There was no movement from the bed, so she edged closer and tried again. "Is your name Ally? Or Sam? I want to help you and get you home to your parents."

The figure moved, just enough to urge Valentina forward. She reached the bed and knelt down, gently pulling the blanket down enough to reveal a little girl's face. The child was dirty, blonde hair knotted with sweat and dried blood. Her cheekbones were bruised, big blue eyes full of tears, lips pressed together tightly in fear.

"I'm not going to hurt you," Valentina promised, not daring to touch the girl and scare her more. "The bad guys brought me here too. Now we're going home."

"Home?" The little girl sat up and sniffled. When the blanket fell back, Valentina saw bruises on the girl's shoulders and prayed there were no more beneath the ratty gray nightgown. "I wanna go home."

Valentina nodded. "We're gonna go home...Ally?" The girl nodded. "Good. Will you come with me?" She held out a hand, and after a moment's hesitation Ally tentatively accepted the her hand and crawled out of bed, clutching a dirt-covered stuffed rabbit.

Together they left the room, only to stop in front of the other door.

"We have to help another person, okay?" Valentina freed her hand from the child's tight grasp and knocked off the doorknob on the second door. Ally clung to her leg as she entered the room.

The boy was huddled in the corner, brown eyes already shooting daggers at Valentina. The look would have amused her at any other time. She wasn't a big fan of kids, but the snarky ones always made her laugh. This one was tough, frightened but courageous all the same.

"Sam?" She stopped at the foot of the bed, taking in the trembling child with torn pants, a dingy white shirt, and tousled hair in need of a trim. He seemed to be favoring his right shoulder. "My name is Tina. I'm going to get you out of here."

"Go away." His voice was small but strong. "You're a bad guy!"

Carefully, Valentina knelt. Ally clutched her shoulder as she did so. "Sam, I'm not a bad guy. They took me too. But I'm going to make sure you get home."

"She's gonna save us," Ally put in, having decided to trust Valentina wholly. "Tina is a good guy."

Sam stared at her warily, wrestling between hope and doubt. "Liar."

"I'm telling the truth." She tried to keep her voice calm, though annoyance bubbled up. "But we don't have much time, Sam. We have to go right now, before the bad guys get back. We have to leave so we can find the police and get help."

The boy's jaw clenched, but the thought of being home again with his dog and toys won over hesitation. He jumped up and ran over, refusing to take her hand while rubbing his shoulder. Valentina didn't see an injury, but didn't have the time to figure out what was wrong.

"Okay, guys, we're going home."

Chapter
SEVENTEEN

THE CHILDREN, NOW freed from their prison, hugged Valentina's sides as they made their way down the hall and one flight of stairs. The walk down the third story was slow, Valentina stymied by her injured leg and Sam holding his aching shoulder gingerly, afraid to let anything or anyone touch him.

When they reached the second floor landing, Valentina's heart nearly stopped. The house in the woods was so quiet that she could hear every noise, and right now, just outside, came the sound of an approaching car. Quickly, she ushered the kids into a nearby room and gestured for them to sit.

"Stay here," she ordered. "I'll be right back. Don't come out no matter what, you hear me?"

"Don't go," Ally whimpered, big tears rolling down her cheeks.

"I have to make sure the bad guys don't find you, okay?" Valentina attempted a comforting smile, knowing she failed miserably. "Now, I don't care what happens or what you hear. You don't move until I come find you, got it?"

She waited until both children gave her hesitant nods before backing out of the room and shutting the door behind her. The looks of terror on their faces pulled at her, but she couldn't let them face who she knew had come for her.

Alan wouldn't go down so easily.

In one hand she held the gun, in the other the pipe. She probably would have better luck with the gun, but she liked the reach and told herself it gave her an advantage. Plus, if the weapon was taken from her during a scuffle, she'd rather defend herself against metal than bullet.

Despite his gangly form and salesman-type appearance, Alan didn't strike Valentina as an adversary who was defeated without a fight. There was strength in that form and evil lurking behind those watery brown eyes. A different kind of evil than Dane – Alan was calm and calculating, the kind of man who knew how to get in someone's head and drive them insane. He didn't see people as human beings. Valentina was just a paycheck to him, and he'd do whatever he had to do to get his money.

Caution mixed with anticipation as she slowly stalked down the hallway – and then turned into a shock of terror when the lights went out.

All of them.

The house was bathed in pitch-black nothingness, the windowless hallway allowing not even the tiniest slivers of moonlight to pierce the dark. A shuddering breath exploded from Valentina's chest as she flattened herself to the wall, sinking down until her butt hit the floor. Somewhere behind her, she heard the children whimper, but thankfully they stayed put.

The wooden paneling scraped her back through her thin shirt, but still she pressed herself harder against the wall, trying to sink into it. Her head screamed at her to run, but where? There was nowhere to go, no way to navigate the house without stumbling along and giving away her location.

And then there was the fear creeping up her spine to

consider as well.

Valentina sat locked against the wall, knees brought up to her chest, chin quivering. All the work she'd put in to not being afraid was forgotten. She couldn't do this, couldn't fight without sight, couldn't escape a dark cage with walls that closed in on her. She couldn't be the hero of her own story, let alone those of children. She just couldn't, not when her nightmare was slowly becoming reality.

Get up.

A voice inside her head demanded the impossible of her. Her legs weren't strong enough to support her trembling body. Her eyes weren't able to open and face the curtain of nothingness.

Get off the fucking floor.

The voice came again, so like her own and yet completely foreign. Valentina wanted to follow that voice, but the coward in her was threatening to take control.

Move!

The last command jolted her upright and she followed without hesitation, climbing to her feet and bracing a hand against the wall. She could have stayed there, pressed against the wall as she listened for the approaching enemy. But, that inner voice knew better, knew that whether she stayed or not, *he* would find her. On the move, at least she could direct attention away from the kids.

Step by step she edged her way through the dark, listening to the sounds on the first floor: a door slamming, footsteps slowly crossing a room, a muttered curse. If the darkness was good for nothing else, at least sound decided to be on her side.

Valentina ducked around a corner and nearly ran face-first into another wall, managing to stop herself by placing a hand out in front of her. She felt her way a few more steps, fingers trembling, breath coming out in quiet shakes of air. In the black screen before her she saw *him*, a dark shadow against the void. She wanted to scream at him, command him to leave as footsteps grew louder below her, but the thought of opening her mouth and forming words seemed an impossible feat. Instead, she did the next-best thing.

She flattened herself against the wall and closed her eyes, pretending she could neither see nor hear The Midnight Man.

In her heart she knew the act was irrational. He would come for her no matter what she did or said. But somehow, pretending to be invisible helped. She could picture herself melting into the wood, becoming one with the wall, blending in so perfectly that the enemy would walk by without ever knowing she even existed. All she had to do was stay put and not move a muscle.

He can't find you.

She repeated the words to herself as she opened her eyes a crack, throat clenching together in panic. Her feet moved toward the stairs, or where she hoped they would be. How long had she been against the wall, convincing herself to move? She'd lost track of time and place, didn't hear any movement downstairs anymore. The house itself groaned and creaked, but she couldn't distinguish natural settling noises from potential movement.

"Fu—"

The curse strangled in her throat when a pair of hands grabbed her shoulders, thrusting her away from the wall. She shrieked out a protest, annoyed that she had somehow been caught in the dark, but the words were shaken out of her. Feebly she struck out with the pipe, first hitting the wall, then connecting with a body part. She didn't know which one, but the sound of a man's grunt told her she at least got one good hit in.

The feeling of triumph didn't last long. Valentina fought against the figure, blindly striking out only to hit air.

But when strong hands captured her wrists and squeezed hard, the fight in her started to fade away.

The weapon fell from Valentina's hand as she tumbled down the stairs, each wooden step connecting painfully with her shoulder, knee, wrist, head... The fall seemed to last longer than it took her to walk up the stairs as her body registered each shock and her mind cursed at every splinter. Blow by blow she bounced until, finally, she hit the landing of the first floor.

For a moment she could only lie there, assessing her wounds. The man's heavy descending footsteps got her moving, though she couldn't stop the grunts of pain, nor the tears that burned in her eyes. Through those tears she saw beams of moonlight shining through the shutters and the few open windows in the living room, offering her some amount of reprieve from the night.

Tasting blood in her mouth, hoping she wasn't bleeding out elsewhere, Valentina crawled across the floor in search of her weapons. Only the moonlight, pale and dim as it was, aided her, though the aid wasn't much. She could only see dark smudges against hard surfaces, not able to distinguish objects.

A foot pressed into her back, crushing her to the floor. Her cheek pressed into the splintered wood. "You are one serious pain in the ass," Alan said, slightly out of breath. He stood over her for a moment, booted heel grinding into her ribcage. "I tried to be nice to you, Miss Tina, but you wouldn't have it."

A scoff escaped before she could stop it. "Because kidnapping and starving someone is so nice," she muttered, mouth chafing against the floor. "Might as well kill me, because I sure as hell am gonna try to kill you."

Alan laughed while leaning over and pressing her farther into the wood. He moved into her line of vision and she saw that he wore a pair of goggles that she guessed were night vision. "You really do have a mouth on you. The boss will have some fun cleaning it out."

"The boss will never touch me," Valentina spat out, shifting suddenly and throwing Alan off-balance. Guided by the moonlight, she lashed out with her good foot and connected with his groin, taking pleasure in the shout of pain that erupted from the man. She scrambled up from the floor, only to be grabbed by the hair from behind and shoved into the opposite wall. Blood ruptured from her bottom lip at the forceful contact.

"You're quick, I'll give you that," he snarled in her ear, yanking off his goggles now that they were in partial moonlight. "I thought for sure you'd turn into a pile of mush when I shut the lights off. Oh, that's right," he continued when she stopped struggling, "I know all about your little fear of the dark."

"Guess your plan backfired," she retorted. "Shouldn't have left me alone in the dark so much."

Alan spun her around, his body pressed to hers and his hands around her throat before she even realized she was facing the other direction. "I wondered what was wrong with you after we brought you in," he growled, his face only inches from hers. Valentina fought his grasp, arching her neck, gasping for air. "You never once asked why. Why we took you, why we were doing all this, why you, why… why…why…" His hands tightened with each word. "I kind of liked that you weren't whiny and didn't cry, respected you for it. But now? You're just pissing me off."

In the moonlight streaming in through the side window, Valentina saw the intent written clearly on his face. He didn't mean for her to make it through this night, boss or no boss. She had only seconds to save herself.

Weapons. She needed to find her weapons, which she'd dropped during her fall down the stairs. Valentina tore her eyes away from Alan to search the floor. A glint of silver caught her attention and she saw the gun against the far wall – too far away.

Nothing was in her reach. She had nothing to defend herself with, and everything, even her own body, was working against her.

Think.

She couldn't think, not with her air supply currently cut off and her body having gone through an emotional and physical beat-down.

What do the movies do?

Movies had heroes with super-human strength and mental capacities. She was just one woman, half-starved and half out of her mind.

You've got hands, moron.

Where were they now? Clamped around Alan's wrists, fighting to free her throat. Valentina kicked at his shins, but he didn't budge. She felt pressure building behind her eyes, lungs burning, throat constricted. Though it pained her to do so, she removed her hands and hung against the wall by his grasp. Then, with what little strength she had, she sent a fist directly up and into his chin.

The sound of teeth smashing together grated her frayed nerves. Alan released her with a shout and she sucked in a breath, her throat raw. Valentina risked a glance up to see blood dripping from Alan's mouth, though she didn't know if he'd bit his tongue or if, she hoped, she'd knocked out a tooth.

She didn't take the time to ask. When he reached for her again, she ducked and sent her head into his gut, ramming him backwards. They both tumbled to the floor, thudding loudly against the wood.

Fire raced up her leg, sending her in a fit of pain. Valentina looked down to see Alan's hand grasping her shin, pressing against the knife wound. He took advantage of her pause and pounced, legs straddling her hips, trapping her hands against her thighs.

"You really think you can get out of here, don't you?" Alan laughed.

Valentina struggled, but his weight had her pinned down. Only her legs had any sort of freedom, though they didn't help her in this position. Instead she focused on subtly moving her hands – or rather, one hand in one particular pocket. "I'll keep trying until you kill me."

"That can be arranged."

If she wasn't lying flat on her back with a deranged kidnapper on top of her, Valentina might have rolled her eyes at the cliché line. But she kept her eyes even with his, still squirming beneath him in an attempt to get away – and hide the movement at her side.

Alan laughed again, the sound creepily hollow. "Still trying, I see. Miss Tina, I've been doing this a long time. Trust me when I say, it won't end well for you."

Valentina stopped struggling, her expression turning almost stoic. "And trust me when I say, this is really gonna hurt."

With a quick flick of the wrist she twisted the knife up and angled it into his groin, slashing upwards when he screamed and slicing the blade sideways until the bunching of his jeans popped the blade from her hand.

The high-pitched wail pierced her ears. Valentina gasped in disgust when she felt blood on her thighs and she shoved herself back on her elbows, crawling out from under Alan. The man was no longer concerned with her as he grasped himself, falling onto his side as sounds of pure agony escaped his gaping mouth. She'd never heard noises like that, and despite knowing she was the cause of them, the wails unnerved her and for a minute she could only stare at the fallen figure who had brought her into this mess. He was trying to say something, to curse at her, but his body was locked in a state of shock for its lost appendage.

"I told you," she finally breathed out, crawling to her knees. "I told you what I'd do if you ever touched me."

Though there was no chance of him getting up, Valentina ran for the gun anyway, nearly collapsing on the floor when she leaned over to retrieve the weapon. She stood on shaky legs, pointing the barrel at Alan. He glared up at her from the floor, knowing better than to speak, his eyes saying what his mouth couldn't. The hate and fury radiating off him surprised Valentina, considering the blood pooling beneath him, and she assumed that whatever adrenaline was keeping him alive was also numbing his body from the pain.

Still, his emotions did nothing to quell her thirst for more blood. By now, after being trapped in that room, deprived of food and light, having everything stripped away from her, she felt only grim satisfaction for what she was about to do.

"You want to know why I never asked 'why me' during all this?" she asked, gesturing with her free hand to the house. "Because it doesn't matter. It doesn't matter why you chose me. It doesn't matter what you wanted. It doesn't matter what you or your boss want to do to me. All that matters is what I've been planning to do all along."

Alan sneered up at her, his face pale, his body shaking. "You don't have it in you. You're just a—"

The gunshot cut off his words as a bullet found its place in his shoulder. She'd been aiming for his chest, but supposed the shoulder would do when shock transformed his expression and the pain registered. There were no more words to be said – he knew he had been defeated. Valentina waited until he collapsed onto his back before approaching him cautiously.

"You made a mistake picking me," she stated, voice empty of emotion. "I know how this ends in the movies, and I don't intend on making any mistakes."

Valentina lifted the gun and fired two shots, both of them connecting with Alan's head. She wasn't taking any chances. She watched enough horror flicks to know what happened next – the bad guy was down, the heroine thinking he was dead and tries to escape, only to have the enemy seemingly rise from the dead to attack again. No, Alan would not be stopping her from escaping. The blood and brain matter on the floor around him was testament to that fact.

For good measure, she unloaded another bullet into the body before her – and stumbled backwards when the sound of her gunfire mixed with another.

Valentina hit the stairs, hand searching for the source of the pain radiating up her shoulder and neck. Her fingers touched wetness, a burning sensation in her upper right arm. A quick glance down showed a bullet wound dark against the moonlight; a glance up had her forgetting her arm and instead attempting to melt into the wooden stairs.

There, in the doorway, framed by the night and moonlight, stood the man who had haunted her for so many years. A wide-brimmed hat shadowed his face, a long coat cloaking a broad build, silver glinting in his hand. His breathing was rough, a warning of what was soon to come.

The Midnight Man had come for her after all.

Unable to see his features, yet trapped by a glare she knew was locked on her, Valentina whimpered. She froze, watching as he entered the house, stepped over Alan, and approached her. Only when he was within reaching distance did she move, scrambling backwards, elbows connecting with wood when he merely kicked out a foot and sent her tumbling back to the floor.

And then, for the first time, The Midnight Man spoke.

"You have caused more trouble than you're worth," he growled, "but you're gonna make it up to me."

His voice was gravelly, sending chills up Valentina's spine. Those chills froze her in place, half on the stairs, legs stretched out in front of her. All her childhood nightmares came rushing to her mind at once, years of terror building in one giant ball of pressure in her chest. She wanted to scream, but his glare had her pinned.

The gun pressed against her head, metal hot against her flesh. "Don't you worry," The Midnight Man breathed into her ear. "I ain't gonna kill you. But by the time I'm done having fun with you, you're gonna wish it all ended right here."

She told herself to fight. He wasn't going to kill her. He wanted her alive, which meant she still had a chance. But not even in her dreams had she ever defied The Midnight Man. Eyes closing in defeat, Valentina could only image what he had planned for her.

He isn't real.

The figure before her most certainly was real. She could feel him, hear him.

He can't hurt you.

The pain in her shoulder said otherwise. Her entire body ached.

You can survive him.

Her eyes snapped open, determination filling them. She could survive. She *would* survive. Fear of the dark, fear of *him*, would no longer control her.

"Okay," she said quietly as she slumped against the stairs. "Okay. Just…don't hurt me anymore. I just… I don't want to be hit or stabbed or shot anymore."

He observed her silently for a moment, standing tall at her feet. She could feel the heat of his gaze from beneath that hat. "Suddenly so compliant," he snarled. "A woman and her tricks."

Valentina sighed. "I'm all out of tricks." She attempted to shift, one arm behind her back and the other holding the bullet wound, but only caused herself more pain. "Just patch me up. Whatever."

If he believed her, or even if he didn't, The Midnight Man didn't react. He simply reached down and grabbed hold of her shirt, pulling Valentina to her feet. His large rough hand clipped her chin in the process, jarring her concentration.

But not enough to stop her from one last try.

When The Midnight Man yanked her against him, Valentina matched his movements and produced her arm from behind her back. In her hand she held the metal pipe, the same pipe that had fallen from her hand and landed on the bottom step, the same pipe she discovered only when the gunshot forced her onto her back, landing on top of it.

The end of that pipe found its way into the back of his head, not enough to harm, but enough that he released her and reached for his wound. Valentina used the momentary distraction to spin on her good leg and wrap her arms around him from behind, pressing the pipe against his throat. She was so short, and he so tall, that she was practically climbing on his back to tighten her grip.

The Midnight Man snarled and reached around, grabbing a chunk of Valentina's short curly hair. His fist tightened, yanking her head forward as both their bodies propelled backwards. He slammed her against the wall, trying to shake her off, but she had better leverage and the lack of oxygen was working in her favor. His free hand grasped at her arms, which were tucked against his throat on either side, the metal crushing his windpipe.

Valentina released the deep-bellied scream that had been building for weeks. Her throaty roar consumed her, sent fire racing through her blood, wrapping around them in a tornado of strength and fury. She didn't notice when the fist entangled in her hair loosened, or when the gasping growls silenced. It wasn't until they both started to slump to the floor that she realized he was unconscious.

Valentina braced herself against the wall and let the other figure slide to his back. In the moonlight she saw a slight rise and fall of his chest. He was still alive.

"No," she whispered, her breath heavy. With jerky, uncoordinated steps she dropped to the floor next to the abandoned gun. She didn't know how many bullets were left, but wasn't going to take any chances.

Valentina pressed the barrel to his temple. A lifetime of memories filled her vision – hiding in the closet from the figure in the dark, pulling the covers over her head to pretend she couldn't see the shadow against the night. She could end it all right here, right now.

But it was different. The gun was against his head. He was still alive. Was it self-defense, or just plain murder? Was she the kind of person who could kill an unconscious man?

He'll do to others what he did to you.

She knew it was true. If he got away, he'd just start over. More children to hurt. More women to sell. More people to kill.

The Midnight Man twitched, his arm flying back and striking her injured leg. Startled, Valentina twitched as well – the gunshot deafening her.

She gasped, eyes wide at the grisly sight in front of her. It was an accident, and yet, she wasn't sorry for it. The mix of blood and brain, the smell of death, made her sick and she fell onto her hands as she vomited next to the body. She retched until her empty stomach could only dry heave and her ribs ground against one another.

When she finally composed herself, Valentina felt a bit clearer, and even a little happy. They were gone. Every last enemy was defeated, if not dead then on the run.

She *won*.

Valentina breathed out a breath mixed with relief and disbelief. Barely able to process that fact, and unable to process everything she'd done to free herself, she told herself to get moving again. She turned her head when she rifled through the man's pockets and found a pair of keys.

That was all she needed.

Tucking the gun in the waistband at her back, Valentina hurried up the stairs and knocked lightly on the room that hid the children.

"Ally? Sam?" She opened the door slowly, then stumbled back when they both tore out of the room and wrapped their arms around her. "Easy," she chuckled. "Let's get out of here."

She led them to the first floor and out the front door, covering their eyes when they passed the bodies. They'd seen enough at this house and she wasn't about to scar them further.

There were two cars in the driveway, the one that had taken her to the house and a dark blue windowless van. It was so cliché that Valentina nearly rolled her eyes, but instead she ushered the kids to the van and got them settled in the front seat. When she climbed into the driver's seat, she stole a glance behind her to ensure the van was empty. Out of the corner of her eye she saw straps, blankets, and boxes, but refused to think what would have happened to her if she'd been forced back there.

"Okay, let's go home," she whispered, starting the van. Part of her couldn't believe she was actually driving away from this horror house; the other part still feared for the immediate future and worried that someone else would show up soon. They were driving down a dark road through the woods, directed only by her memory, searching for civilization when she didn't even know what state she was in, let alone the town.

She drove slowly, unfamiliar with the narrow road surrounded by woodland. The headlights reached out before her, lighting a frightening path into darkness.

Valentina had never been much for prayer, but she silently prayed for dawn and an end to the night. She missed sunlight, warmth, the feeling of life energizing her body.

The children curled up against one another, eyes already drooping. Ally had her bunny clutched to her chest, and Sam had his arm around them both. If not for the bruises, dirt, and dried blood covering them both, Valentina would have said the scene was bordering on adorable. She smiled softly after looking them over, then turned her eyes back to the road. Exhaustion racked her body as much as it did theirs, but she couldn't afford to let fatigue take over now.

Valentina allowed a single yawn before sitting up straight and gripping the wheel tighter. She realized she should have grabbed something to eat or drink before they left, but she'd been so focused on getting out of that house that such things didn't even cross her mind.

I can eat later, she told herself, taking deep breaths as though to remind herself that she was still alive. *Get to civilization first.*

She remembered the drive being long when she'd been trapped in the trunk, and this time was no different. Night turned to dawn as the van crunched over gravel and twigs. Valentina stifled another yawn, and then another, letting her eyes adjust to the first light she'd seen in days, perhaps even weeks.

It was beautiful.

Her eyes watered, not from pain, but from the joy of such freedom. Valentina sniffled and blinked the tears back. Her hands shook from hunger and tiredness, and the lull of the drive threatened to put her to sleep. She'd lost so much blood that her mind was getting foggy, but she let the sun fuel her forward mile by mile.

Later, she wouldn't remember the rest of the drive, not the feel of the road or the joy of dawn. But she would remember the relief she felt when, finally, she saw signs of life.

The wooded path ended at some kind of back road. She racked her memory trying to remember which way they'd turned, but at this point, her mind was too far gone to comprehend direction. She took a best guess and headed left. Excitement began to uncurl in her belly at the thought of people – and food.

Sam stirred at the change in direction, blinking in the morning light. "Are we there yet?"

Valentina huffed out a laugh at the innocence in his question. "Soon," she replied quietly, hoping she wasn't telling a lie.

Before long both kids were awake, though they stayed silent. Valentina stole a couple quick glances in their direction. They were tired, but something else haunted their expressions…and she didn't want to know what it was. She supposed it was wrong of her to feel that way, but Valentina wasn't sure she could handle knowing the details of what those two troubled, pure, and unlucky souls had experienced.

But she could offer some semblance of comfort. Valentina gave them both a smile, then reached out and offered her right hand. After a moment's hesitation, Sam took her palm and held it in his lap, while Ally wrapped herself around her arm. A sudden stabbing pain in her shoulder reminded Valentina of the bullet wound she'd not-so-skillfully covered with a piece of cloth, but she allowed the kids to cling to her anyway. They sat that way for another hour, seeing no other cars on the road.

Until she reached the end.

Valentina pulled up at a stop sign, slowing the van and searching their surroundings. Straight ahead was another road in the woods, but to the right she saw the very edge of rooftops. Homes? Restaurants? Police station? She wasn't sure, but she directed the van in that direction nonetheless.

"Oh, thank god," Valentina whispered when the outskirts of a small town came into view. The main road was narrow, but lined with small buildings. After she saw the flashing "diner" sign, she didn't even care what the rest of them were.

Nor did she care about proper parking. She drove the van up to the diner and parked in the middle of the road, gesturing for the kids to follow her out the driver's side door. They hopped out behind her but stayed close, Ally begging to be picked up while Sam clutched her leg. With what little effort she had left, Valentina hoisted the frail girl up and settled her on her left hip, then slowly walked toward the diner. A smile broke out on her face when she peered through the glass to see three police offers settled on the barstools at the counter.

That smile dropped when she heard a shout behind her. The trio turned to see an old man standing down the sidewalk pointing. Valentina, ready to pass out as it was, couldn't make out his words, only his frantic tone and shaking hand. He continued to yell, catching the attention of those around them – including the police officers in the diner.

"What?" Valentina asked, mostly to herself. She took a step close to the man, who stumbled back at the movement. "I... What's wrong?"

The old man shouted again, still pointing. He seemed to be gesturing to something behind her, something *on* her. Valentina ran a hand down her shirt, not feeling anything other than dried blood and sweat on her clothes. Then her fingers touched something cold at her back, and she realized what the man was shouting.

Gun.

And not just any gun, either. It was the kind of gun only bad guys carried, the kind that no one should be authorized to carry, especially with two children so close at hand. But she hardly registered that thought as she pulled the gun from her waistband, holding it in front of her. For a moment she stared down at the weapon, not even remembering tucking it into her pants.

Another shout, this one deeper and with more authority, had Valentina turning again. This time the policemen faced her, two with their guns drawn and the third holding out a hand as though pleading with her.

"What?" she asked again, blinking slowly, the side of her head pressed against Ally's forehead as the child tightened her hold. She still held the gun in her free hand, and when the officer took a step closer, her grip tightened.

Protect what's yours.

Another person who wanted to contain her. Another man who looked at her like she was something to be destroyed.

"Are you one of them?" she asked, her voice stronger than she felt. "Are you part of it?"

The officer paused, brows knitting together in confusion as he looked over the filthy woman with blood staining her cheeks. He glanced over his shoulder at the other two deputies, who maintained their gun-drawn stances but also shared the same cautious expression. "Part of what?"

"You're not taking us back," Valentina continued, not hearing him speak. "I'm taking the kids home. You won't stop me."

"Calm down, ma'am," the man said softly, not coming any closer. "I'm not…"

Then he stopped, standing up a little straighter. "Are you…Valentina Murdoch?"

At the sound of her name, something woke up in Valentina. Clarity focused her senses. "You…you know me?"

"You're the Valentina who went missing three weeks ago? Is this Ally Jameson and Samuel Beckens?"

She tightened her hold. "Maybe."

The officer laughed, surprising Valentina. "We have been looking for you for weeks. You're safe now. Valentina, put down the gun."

Relief flooded through her, but she couldn't let go.

"Valentina, put down the gun."

Was she free? Was the nightmare over? Her hand trembled as much as the children's entire bodies did.

"Where am I?"

"…Cransville."

It took her a moment, but she finally placed the name – a town that was three hours from her own.

"I need to call my family."

"We'll take care of you. But you have to put down the gun."

She thought she'd already done that, but now the request seemed so hard. The gun had protected her, saved her life. It was the weapon that ended the life of true terrorists. To give up the one thing keeping her safe… She wasn't sure she could do that. Not now.

Let it go, idiot.

Valentina blew out a breath and let the gun fall to the pavement. The policemen rushed forward, one of them kicking away the weapon and the other two reaching for the kids. Both Ally and Sam screamed when the men touched them, grabbing hold of Valentina in a death grip.

"Just take us somewhere safe," she requested, unable to bear their cries. "Let us go home."

Chapter
Eighteen

THE OFFICERS TOOK the trio to the hospital, frantically making phone calls during the short drive. Valentina didn't even attempt to listen, though she was aware of the bustle of activity along the street. The cops seemed to know who to call for each of them, and she let them do their job, too miserable by the thought of not being able to call Leo to object to them taking charge.

Ally and Sam slept on either side of her. She had one arm around Sam, the other at her side. Only when they arrived at the ER did she rustle them from their slumber. They entered the hospital together and were taken to the same room, as the children refused to detach themselves. Valentina could only shrug and smile wearily at the nurses, who brought in two extra beds. The room was surprisingly spacious, a welcomed sight from her small wood-paneled cell.

Valentina convinced the kids to each take a bed and let the doctors look them over. She heard them crying as the curtains were pulled for privacy, but right now she needed to let the doctors take care of them. So, she focused on the two nurses and one doctor in her own curtained-off section.

"Alright," one of them said softly. The name *Jen* was embroidered on her coat. "We need to do a full medical

workup, and I need you to be completely honest with me."
Valentina nodded, shoulders slumped. "Were you sexually
assaulted? Are you sure?" the nurse pressed when Valentina
shook her head.

"Yeah, I'm sure. He tried, but I killed him."

Jen glanced up at that, her face expressionless at the
other woman's deadpan tone. "Where is all this blood
coming from?"

Valentina shrugged again. "Not all of it is mine. I have
a bad leg cut," she gestured to her leg, wincing slightly, "and
a guy shot me here." She pointed to her arm. "Other than
that it's just cuts and bruises, I think."

Her attention shot to the section next to her when Ally
screamed. "Look," she said, her voice low, "those kids have
been through worse than me. I don't know what that sick
fuck did to them, but whatever it was, you need to focus on
them more than me."

"We will take care of them," the doctor promised, "but
we need to take care of you too."

With a sigh, Valentina relented and fell back on the bed
when they directed her to lie down. She barely felt them
inserting the IV or stitching her up, but was acutely aware
of the sobs coming from the little girl whose innocence had
been stolen from her.

BY THE TIME the doctors finished with the three, the
media had caught wind of the rescue. Valentina could
hear the nurses chatting about the reporters just outside
the ER doors, as none were allowed to enter the hospital.
Policemen came and went, asking questions, writing down
directions, congratulating her on saving herself and the
kids.

Valentina didn't feel like a hero. She should have done

more, and done it sooner. But, she could be thankful that she was alive, and that her family was coming to bring her home. The police had only said "family" was on their way, and she guessed that meant her mother, and maybe Slim.

For now, she leaned back against her propped-up hospital bed hooked up to an IV and eating a cheeseburger with French fries. The kids had been given their requests of chocolate ice cream and pizza. Food had never tasted better, though she had to eat slowly, and couldn't finish the meal. What she really wanted was to shower and sleep, but Valentina refused to let the kids out of her sight until they were safely in their parents' arms.

That time came sooner than she expected.

The door to their room opened and four adults rushed in, led by a police officer. Two sets of parents skimmed the room quickly before their eyes landed on the children.

"Mommy!" Ally shouted just as Sam called out for his own.

Valentina watched as the parents rushed over, tears streaming down their cheeks. They collected the kids from the bed, hugging them tightly, whispering words of love into their ears. Ally's mother sank to the floor, her daughter in her arms, rocking back and forth as the pair sobbed together. Sam had been collected onto his father's lap in a chair in the corner, his mother kneeling with her arms around them both.

Valentina took in the scene with a sad smile, happy that the children were back with their parents but heartbroken that their reunion had to be because of something so tragic. She didn't have long to ponder such thoughts, though, for an officer approached her bed and placed a hand on her shoulder.

"You did good," he said, nodding down at her. "And I thought you'd like to know that your family arrived."

She didn't take her eyes off the scene before her when

she asked, "Who?"

"Your mother and your husband."

Her eyes tore away from the children to bore into the officer. So many questions flooded her mind, but before she could formulate even half of one, the door opened again and in walked the man she thought to be dead.

"Leo," Valentina whispered, her voice breaking on the second syllable. She barely had time to shift before the two had crossed the room and Leo swept her off the bed.

"Jesus Christ, Val," Leo whispered in her ear, words choked with tears. "I thought I lost you."

"Lost me?" she repeated, not able to pull away. "They told me they killed you. I… I thought you were dead."

Leo drew back just enough to touch his forehead to hers. "The son of a bitch tried, but I guess I'm made of tougher stock than that. He got away, but the police are searching for him."

Valentina sniffled. "I… I got the others."

His expression changed to curiosity, but Lillian interrupted his next question. She all but crushed her daughter against her, hands moving up and down her daughter's back as though to check she was actually there. "Oh, honey. I was so scared. I was so scared. I'm so sorry."

"It's not your fault, Mom," Valentina whispered, taking in the comforting and familiar scent of her mother's shampoo. "I'm back now, and in one piece."

"What happened?" Lillian asked, brushing back her daughter's hair. "What did they do to you?"

"How did you get out? What's with the kids?" Leo put in.

Valentina couldn't help but laugh. "There's time for all that. Right now I want to go home, take a shower, and just sleep for the next week."

Leo grinned and kissed her, careful to avoid the cuts on her face. "Whatever you want, babe. Just know that MoMo is going to demand attention as soon as you walk through the door."

The name elated her. "He's okay? I thought maybe he got out when…"

"He's fine," Leo assured her, taking her chin in his hand when her expression fell. "We're fine."

She started to reply, but turned instead when she sensed someone approaching. The parents she identified as Ally's stood on one side of the bed, Sam's on the other.

"We just wanted to say thank you," Ally's mother said, hands clutching together nervously. Her husband put an arm around her shoulder, the other holding Ally.

"We know there's nothing we could ever say or do to show how much we appreciate you rescuing our little girl," he added, "but if you ever need anything, you just let us know."

Sam's mother reached over and hugged her gently. "The same goes for us. What you did…you're our hero."

Valentina swallowed back tears and smiled. "I'm glad I was there for them."

And she meant it.

Leo watched the adults as they turned back to their kids and began talking with the doctors and police. The children refused to let go of their parents, but cast several glances and waves over at Valentina, who made silly faces back at them to get them giggling.

He nudged her shoulder playfully. "So…you want one?"

Valentina turned her gaze up to her husband. "Not even a little bit."

Leo laughed and slid an arm around her shoulders. "That's my girl."

Chapter NINETEEN

TWO DAYS LATER, after countless tests, IVs filled with fluids, many bandage changes, and a long discussion with the police, Valentina was allowed to go home.

She didn't remember much of the previous couple days. She'd requested to go home immediately, but the doctors refused, instead wanting to keep her for observation. Her body was severely dehydrated and emaciated, her leg wound infected. Luckily the bullet wound wasn't serious, though it hurt like hell. The nurses visited her room often to check up on her, while Leo and her mother fed her constantly. After a while, Valentina tried to sleep, but the thought of getting to go home and rest in her own bed, where she was safe, kept her up throughout the night. She passed the hours by watching late-night sitcoms on the small hospital room TV, needing something to fill the silence while her loved ones slept in the chairs on either side of her.

But now she was on her way home – back to where it all began, and yet, back to where she felt safest.

Lillian drove, Valentina curled up in the backseat against her husband. Having thought he was dead, murdered because of her, she had a hard time letting go of his hand. Leo spoke softly to her during the drive, telling her about the jogger who came forward, his time spent with the local police, and of his fight with Johnny, who now had his picture plastered on the *wanted* posters and was being hunted night and day.

Valentina knew why. Johnny was the last tie to whatever operation Alan and Dane were part of. He was the only one who could give the police the information they needed to stop the chain of human trafficking. Part of her hoped it ended with the men she killed back at the house, but she knew better than that. They were part of something bigger, just one small section wiped off the grid. She supposed she should feel guilty about killing rather than simply incapacitating the bad guys so that the cops could have questioned them, but when she really thought about it, she didn't feel bad at all.

They deserved exactly what they got.

BY THE TIME they made it home, dodging the reporters camped out at the end of their driveway, Valentina was nearly comatose. The closer they got to home, the more she felt the weight of the past few weeks.

Lillian ushered her inside while Leo fended off the reporters begging for exclusive interviews. Once the door was locked behind them, Valentina felt slender arms wrap around her and heard Slim's voice in her ear.

"It's okay, Slim," she told her friend, who was trying her hardest not to cry. "Hey," she pulled back and smiled, "it's okay. And thank you, for everything." Leo had told her what Slim and Dom offered for the reward money, and she was touched by their gesture.

"Girl, I'd do and give anything for you," Slim replied, wiping her eyes and stepping to the side when Dom grabbed Valentina into a hug.

"Good to have you back," he said, his hug warm and

tender. "Now go take a shower. You smell."

"Dom!" Slim and Leo both exclaimed, but Valentina only laughed. The laugh came from deep down and bubbled up, a true laugh that felt fantastic. After a pause, the others joined in and they allowed themselves a moment to celebrate.

"Shower it is," Valentina finally managed around one last chuckle.

"And then bed," Leo added. Slim and Dom took the hint and said their good-byes, promising to come back tomorrow.

While Lillian went to prepare the bedroom, Leo started the shower and helped Valentina undress, setting out the bandages they would have to replace afterward. When she stood naked before him, he had to force himself to keep a calm face.

She'd lost a lot of weight, bones sticking out that hadn't been visible before. But more distracting than that were the bruises marring her flesh. Black marks covered her ribs and hips, bruises in the shape of fingers on her throat and shoulders. Her injured leg was slightly swollen, twenty stitches sealing together the knife wound. Sutures also stretched across her right upper arm where the bullet had passed through. One side of her face was red, her eye bruised, lower lip scabbed.

She was broken in every sense of the word, and he was going to put her back together again.

"Easy," Leo directed as he helped her into the shower, joining her under the hot water. He soaped up a washcloth and wiped it across her shoulders and chest, wringing out water that turned black beneath the spray. Weeks-old blood and dirt flushed across the blue tile and down the drain.

Valentina let him wash her, comforted by the feel of his hands, the warmth of the water. She could have fallen asleep right there, leaning against him, but a sudden thought had her pulling back. "Hey…whatever happened with that agent?"

When Leo didn't respond, she sighed. "I screwed it up, didn't I?"

"Hey," he said sharply, forcing her to meet his gaze. "You didn't screw up anything. You got that?" Valentina nodded, so he continued to wipe away the grime from her skin. "But…I thought it was over that day. I ran out of there when Slim called and didn't wait around to tell the agent since she was in the bathroom. To be honest, I didn't think anything else of it because I was so focused on getting you back. Then she called about two weeks later and said she understood, and that she hoped everything worked out, and to give her a call again when I had you back safe and sound."

Valentina lifted her head, a ghost of a smile playing at her chapped lips. "So you get a second chance?"

"Sounds like it." Leo kissed her forehead. "And I think I'm gonna pitch a new book about one hell of a woman who beat the odds, kicked some bad guy ass, and saved a couple of kids while doing so."

They fell into a comfortable, familiar silence after that, Valentina leaning against her husband, Leo gently cleaning her. After a while he moved to her hair, running his fingers through the knots and shampooing out the scent of death and decay. Steam surrounded them in a protective haze, the sound of the water soothing away tension and stress.

When Valentina sighed softly and rested her head against his shoulder, Leo set down the washcloth. "I love you, Val."

"I love you too," she whispered back. The simple but all-too-meaningful words released the locks she'd bolted inside herself and she finally gave in to everything she'd felt the past three weeks.

Wrapping her arms around Leo, feeling his strong

arms do the same, Valentina wept. She cried the tears she'd refused to let fall except over Leo's supposed death; she cried for herself, for Ally and Sam, for her family, for everyone who had been taken before her and never got to see their loved ones again. She cried simply because she was exhausted and hurt and wanted one moment to feel sorry for herself.

Leo let her have that moment, not saying a word, understanding her need to release everything that had built up inside her. Her sobs eventually faded, so he shut off the water and dried them both off, then skillfully bandaged up her wounds.

When she was clean and cared for, he carried her to the bed and stretched out beside her, nodding to Lillian as she smiled over at them before closing the door, giving them their privacy on the night they needed it most.

Leo reached out and ran his hand down her hair, marveling at the feel of her skin beneath his hand. They stared at one another, both unable to express the meaning behind their reunion. They stared until Valentina's eyes began to droop and she offered a sigh of contentment.

Leo pulled the comforter up to her chin. "Sleep," he said softly. "You're home. You're safe."

Valentina smiled lightly, curling her legs up and closing her eyes. "Leo?"

"Yes?"

"Can you turn off the light?"

Leo frowned, surprised by the request, but did as asked. He clicked off the nightlight on her side of the bed, waiting for her to panic when the room was cloaked in darkness. But she didn't. Instead, she settled down farther into the blanket, murmuring a satisfied breath when he molded his body to hers and held her against him with a comforting arm.

And for the first time since childhood, Valentina slept

without fear of The Midnight Man.

A Special Thanks To

Samantha, for inspiring the tough and brave Valentina Murdoch. One day we'll be neighbors who talk books and botanicals and Boardwalk Empire all day long.

Kristi Strong, for reading early versions of the book and offering advice. I don't know what I'd do without you!

Donna Dull, for taking on the most confusing thing in the world to me: formatting! Your talents impress me on a daily basis.

My family, for helping me every step of the way. As corny as it sounds, I truly wouldn't be here without you.

My husband, Seth, for putting up with my constant book chatter that I'm sure makes no sense. But you listen anyway, and that's all that matters.

Readers, all of you! Whether you love my books or hate them, I'm honored that you give up your time to read my words.

About the Author

Night owl, Dorito lover, and quiet eccentric - Kristina Circelli is the author of several fiction novels, including The Helping Hands series, The Whisper Legacy, The Never, and The Sour Orange Derby.

A descendent of the Cherokee nation and niece of a Cherokee elder, Circelli holds both a Bachelor of Arts and Master of Arts in English from the University of North Florida, where she teaches creative writing. She also heads Red Road Editing, a full-service editing company for independent authors and commercial clients.

She currently resides in Jacksonville, Florida with her husband, Seth, and cats, Lord Finnegin the Fierce and Mr. Malachi the Mighty.

Website: www.circelli.info
Email: Kristina@circelli.info
Blog: http://anawfullybigadventure-kc.blogspot.com/
Facebook: Circelli Books - Novels by Kristina Circelli
Twitter: @KCircelli